Two can play at that game.

I flicked my eyes around the restaurant. The two girls at the table to my left weren't looking at me. But they weren't talking to each other either. They had probably heard the whole thing. Even my little fight with Kristin. They were probably just waiting for me to leave so they could start gabbing.

Well, let them wait. I wasn't going to rush out of there like I was all upset. Nobody was going to see me sweat.

A few minutes later I saw Gel on the sidewalk outside, climbing into his car. Just in case I wasn't watching, he pulled out fast enough to make his tires squeal so I'd have to notice him.

It was almost funny. Almost. But not really.

I figured Gel would last maybe twenty-four hours on his own. He might even work up the nerve to call some other girl. When he got the big turndown, he'd come running back.

And I'd take him back. But not right away.

I wanted to see *him* sweat.

Don't miss any of the books in SWEET VALLEY JUNIOR HIGH, an exciting new series from Bantam Books!

Lacey's Crush

Written by
Jamie Suzanne

Created by
FRANCINE PASCAL

BANTAM BOOKS
NEW YORK · TORONTO · LONDON · SYDNEY · AUCKLAND

RL 4, 008-012

LACEY'S CRUSH

A Bantam Book / July 1999

*Sweet Valley Junior High is a trademark of
Francine Pascal.*

Conceived by Francine Pascal.

*Produced by 17th Street Productions,
a division of Daniel Weiss Associates, Inc.
33 West 17th Street, New York, NY 10011.*

ISBN: 0-553-48665-9

Published simultaneously in the United States and Canada

Bantam Books are published by Bantam Books, a division of Random
House, Inc. Its trademark, consisting of the words "Bantam Books" and
the portrayal of a rooster, is Registered in the U.S. Patent and Trademark
Office and in other countries. Marca Registrada. Bantam Books, 1540
Broadway, New York, New York 10036.

PRINTED IN THE UNITED STATES OF AMERICA

OPM   0 9 8 7 6 5 4 3 2 1

To Matthew Joseph Sarafa

Lacey

"You're up early," my dad commented when I came downstairs and slouched in the kitchen doorway. Gathered around the white Formica table were my dad, my stepmother, Victoria, and my half sister, Penelope. All dressed in their tennis whites, eating poached eggs. A painful sight first thing in the morning, believe me. They were so clean and white and perky. It was blinding.

Actually, it was almost noon. But it was early for me. I usually wait until they're gone before I get up on Saturdays. It keeps me sane.

"Where are you going?" Victoria demanded as I did a 180-degree turn. "Don't you want any brunch?"

Brunch with the family? Don't tempt me.

"Out," I answered, heading for the front door.

"When we're finished with our lessons at the club, we need you to watch Penelope for a while," Victoria called back. "We're going to an art gallery."

1

How cultured. Victoria is a real art head. Apparently she has great taste.

"Did you hear that, Lacey?" my dad bellowed. I leaned against the front door, my hand on the door handle, waiting until they were through so I could go. "We'll drop her off about two o'clock," he added.

Outside I heard the familiar rumble of Gel's car. He beeped the horn, and I winced, hoping Victoria hadn't noticed. I mean, Gel can be pretty tacky sometimes. And I really did not need a lecture on my taste in boyfriends just then.

"Are you done?" I yelled out to my dad.

"There's no need for that tone . . . ," he answered.

But I was already out the door.

"This car is so gross," I said to Gel as I got in. I had to push aside a stack of comics, an empty soda can, and a half-empty bag of sour-cream-and-onion potato chips just to sit down. "So, what's the big deal?" I asked, slamming the rust-encrusted door.

Gel had called me that morning to see if I wanted to go to Vito's Pizza for lunch. It's not that I mind getting out of the house—obviously. It's just that Gel has never asked me to lunch, *ever*. In fact, since we've been going out, he's hardly asked me *anything* other than, "Got a light?"

2

"Got a light?" Gel asked as he backed out of our driveway.

I handed him my Bic and fumbled in my purse for my own cigarettes.

Squeak. I jumped. A little blue rubber bunny stared up at me.

One of Penelope's favorite things is to hide her toys in my bag and "surprise" me. She is such a pest.

I took the lighter out of Gel's hands and snagged one of his cigarettes since I couldn't find mine. I didn't light up until we'd made it to the corner, though. My dad and Victoria have enough to complain about. They didn't need to see me smoking.

"I'm beat." Gel sighed, resting his head against the seat back.

Gel was making conversation? I hope he doesn't pull a brain muscle.

Really. Gel is so thick sometimes, he forgets where he's going. Luckily I'm there to remind him.

"Vito's is that way," I pointed out as Gel turned right down the wrong street. "You should've kept going straight."

Gel shrugged and ashed out the open window. "I wanted to finish this smoke," he said, glancing at me.

I shrugged back. I didn't care how far out of

the way we went. I wouldn't care if we drove right out of Sweet Valley. In fact, I wished we would. But that would be too imaginative for Gel—he never surprised me.

No wonder Gel and I never have lunch together—I was getting bored already. As soon as we were done at Vito's, I'd call Kristin to come over while I baby-sat. That way I wouldn't have to suffer the torture solo. Kristin would help me out. That's what best friends are for.

Jessica

"Does my hair look okay?" I asked Elizabeth on the way to Vito's. She was meeting her friends Anna Wang and Salvador del Valle, and I was meeting Kristin Seltzer.

"Elizabeth?" But she kept on walking, her neat blond hair hanging straight down her back, ignoring me.

Useless! Sometimes my twin sister is just useless. I stomped past her until I was in front of a shop window that I could use as a mirror.

I met Elizabeth's gaze in the reflection. "Would you relax?" she said. "You look great. You always do. Come on."

I smiled. She was right—I did look great. Sisters are the best.

I'm not usually self-conscious, but you never know who you might bump into at Vito's.

Vito's is *the* place to be on Saturday. I knew I'd see a lot of people from school there, and I wanted to make a good impression.

At Sweet Valley Middle School, I was popular.

In fact, I would have ruled the school this year. Except that over the summer they decided to re-zone our school district, and Elizabeth and I were transferred to Sweet Valley Junior High.

Since then, I haven't exactly been queen of the social scene.

I wanted that to change.

We walked into Vito's, and I glanced around. I didn't see Kristin anywhere. But I saw Lacey Frells sitting in a booth near the window with her boyfriend, Gel. (He's in high school. I mean, can you *get* much cooler?)

Lacey is Kristin's best friend, and she's beyond cool. Too cool to even care about popularity. Too cool to care if you like her or not. But so cool that being seen with her is kind of an honor.

But Lacey and I hadn't exactly gotten off on the right foot.

Okay, she hates me. But that's another story.

Lacey was holding an unlit cigarette. Probably annoyed that she couldn't smoke inside. She squinted at me. I bit my lip.

Kristin hadn't *said* anything about Lacey joining us. But maybe I was supposed to *assume* that she was. I gave Lacey a couple of seconds to signal me. But she just gave me this level stare.

My palms were getting sweaty. I didn't know what to do.

Elizabeth must have seen my problem. "There's Anna and Salvador," she said softly. "Want to sit with us until Kristin gets here?"

I really didn't want to sit with them. Salvador always makes these obnoxious wisecracks, and Anna is just the opposite—serious and intense. Already Salvador had two straws up his nose, as if he was trying to get a laugh out of Anna. But she just twirled her long black hair between her fingers and stuck out her tongue at him. Why Elizabeth couldn't seem to get enough of those two was beyond me.

Fortunately that's when Kristin came cruising in the door.

"Have fun, you guys," Elizabeth said as she went to sit down with her friends.

"Hi, Jessica. Sorry I'm late," Kristin said breathlessly. She flashed me a smile warm enough to break the weirdness barrier. "Come on. Let's sit down," she added.

I followed Kristin through the restaurant. But when she stopped at Lacey and Gel's booth, I stood slightly apart. I didn't know whether Kristin was planning to sit down with them or not.

"Hey, Lace! How ya doing, Gel?" Kristin said.

Lacey and Gel gazed at us for a few moments. Like they were too cool to recognize us right away. "Hi," both of them finally managed.

Kristin looked a little surprised. After all, she is Lacey's best friend. She was probably used to being greeted in a slightly more friendly way.

Lacey gave me a pointed glare, then looked at Kristin and lifted her brows as if to say, "What's this all about?"

Suddenly I realized what was going on. Lacey hadn't known that Kristin and I were having lunch together. And she *wasn't* happy about it.

I saw Kristin's face tighten a little. But she ignored the chill in the air. "Well, see you guys later."

We hunted around for a booth, but all the booths on Lacey's side of the restaurant were full.

"Come on," Kristin said. "Let's see if there's one on the other side."

"Okay," I chirped, trying to keep the mood light.

As soon as we plopped down in an empty booth in the corner, Kristin leaned forward and swiped her blond curls out of her eyes.

"So," she said, her blue eyes shining. "How are we going to get you and Damon Ross together?"

I blushed.

Damon is this incredibly gorgeous guy in our

class. Brown hair. Blue eyes. Built like a football player—although he wasn't on any teams at school. I had a huge crush on him, but I had absolutely no idea how he felt about me.

"I don't know," I said eagerly. "I keep looking for him, you know, after track practice—like, hanging around the gym or at the mall. He's just never there."

"I wonder what he does," Kristin mused. "He came in halfway through last year. So no one really knows that much about him. And he hardly talks to anyone either."

"*Tell* me about it," I agreed. I'd been trying to talk to Damon for weeks, but something always got in the way. Usually it was my own tongue.

"Maybe he's a snob," Kristin suggested.

I thought about this. Damon a snob?

But what about the time when Damon had silently rescued me from those jerks who were trying to squirt shaving cream in my locker?

Or the time he'd helped me get Lacey's sister's toy rabbit back from some guys playing keep away with it at the mall (while Lacey stood idly by)?

Not too long ago, I'd found a note in my locker wishing me luck at a track meet. *"Run fast as a rabbit,"* it had said. The letter could have been from anybody, and the rabbit reference might have been completely coincidental. But I was pretty sure the note was from Damon.

Damon might be totally aloof, but he was no snob.

"I don't think so," I disagreed, shaking my head. "Maybe he's just really shy."

"He's the *mystery man*," Kristin said, giggling. "Jessica, I think you've found a mission. You *have* to find out more about Damon."

"Right," I said, blowing out a frustrated breath. I leaned back in the booth as the waitress came to take our order.

I was *dying* to find out more about Damon. But how was I going to do it?

Damon

It was such a nice day. Instead of jogging straight back home when I got to the school—the midway point in my weekend runs—I started to walk. I had a couple of hours before I had to get back anyway. And I was a little sick of rushing home all the time. It felt good to just stroll along.

In the field behind the school I could see the football team, running through their drills. I stopped to watch for a second. I'd played football every year at my old middle school back east, but there was no time now. The SVJH team looked pretty good.

After-school sports are pretty much out of the question. My mom's waitressing shift starts at five, so I have to get home by four-thirty to baby-sit my little sisters, Kaia and Sally. I can't make the morning practices during the week either because I have to make breakfast for my sisters too. My mom works really late, so she needs to get as much sleep as she can fit in. I let

11

my sisters wake her up every morning just before I take off for school. They're really funny about it. They sneak into her room and crawl under the covers, and then they start tickling her like crazy. My mom always laughs. I guess it's a good way to wake up—laughing.

I miss football. But my family has a routine going that seems to work well for everybody.

I can't complain.

I kept on walking. Past the little stores on Redwood Street. Down Kane.

I stopped to look in the window of Vinyl, the record store that specializes in old stuff. I really like some of that surf music from the sixties. And now that I'm in California, it's appropriate. But all we have is a portable radio-cassette player with an old Barney tape stuck in it, so you can't use the tape deck anymore.

I kept walking.

Across the street was Vito's Pizza. I could smell garlic and tomatoes, and my stomach started going nuts.

I stopped for a second.

Vito's is always such a scene, and I wasn't sure I could deal with a big crowd of kids from school. But since I always stick pretty much to myself, it's not likely anyone would even notice me.

I had a couple of bucks on me. I could just grab a slice, I thought. It wouldn't take long.

I crossed the street, jogged up the steps, and opened the door.

The restaurant looked busy.

Who knows, I thought, getting my hopes up as I went in.

Maybe I'll see Jessica.

Gel's Six Reasons to Break Up with Lacey

1. She always takes my cigarettes.
2. It's a pain picking her up from school and stuff all the time.
3. She keeps saying my car is gross.
4. She doesn't play video games.
5. She doesn't like Jim Squalor, who is _the_ best DJ in the world.
6. There's this other girl, Gina, from the arcade — she even beat me at Deathstar.

(Lacey probably won't let me break up with her anyway.)

Jessica

Why is it that every time you talk about someone, they seem to appear out of nowhere?

Damon came in and sat down in a booth right across from us.

Kristin was so shocked, she had to spit her soda back into her glass. I could feel my face burning.

He was wearing a plain white T-shirt and navy blue sweatpants, but he still looked adorable. Even his profile was adorable.

Kristin waggled her eyebrows, giving me the universally recognized signal for "what a babe!"

It was unavoidable: I started to giggle. Automatically my hands clamped over my mouth to muffle the sound. If Damon heard me, I'd die, but I was unstoppable.

Kristin laughed too, silently. Her eyes were tearing.

The more I tried to hold my laughter in, the

15

harder it became. Then I heard myself let out this huge—oh my God—*snort*.

Kristin's eyes got so wide, she looked like she was going to explode.

Okay. That was it. Time to get a grip. I wasn't going to just sit there and giggle like some fifth-grader. And I didn't want Damon Ross to think I was some kind of pig.

I was going to get up and say hello to Damon on my way to the bathroom.

I took a deep breath, slid down my seat, and stood up.

"Excuse me," I said to Kristin in my most composed voice.

She cleared her throat and nodded encouragingly at me.

I took a few steps toward Damon's table.

He turned around and smiled this perfect smile when he saw me coming.

"Hey, Jessica," he said.

I smiled back.

"Hey!" I shouted as my heel slipped on something slimy on the floor. Before I knew it, my feet slid out from under me and I was sailing through the air toward the floor. I fell on my side with a big thud in some incredibly gross gunk.

Spaghetti sauce!

Naturally, people in the restaurant started applauding and hooting.

Naturally, I wanted to die.

I was practically lying at Damon's feet.

"Are you okay? Are you okay?" Kristin was squatting down next to me.

"Jess!" Elizabeth appeared immediately. She gave me her hand, like she was going to pull me up.

"Wait!" Damon called. He stooped down and put his hand on my shoulder to keep me from moving. "Make sure you're not hurt before you get up."

I took a few breaths and tried to focus on something other than the warmth of his hand and his amazing blue eyes.

Was anything hurting me?

Yeah. My pride. I was totally humiliated. I'd wiped out right in front of Damon—the most gorgeous guy in the whole world.

My throat felt weird. I'd just die if I started crying!

Everybody was staring at me.

"Bend your knee. Flex your foot," Elizabeth ordered.

I did. Everything was fine.

"I'm okay," I said. "Thanks." My voice sounded shaky. I was trying my best not to burst into tears.

Damon helped me to my feet. My khaki capri pants were splattered with red sauce.

"Come on," Kristin said. "Let's go in the ladies' room. You can get cleaned up."

I practically ran over her to get there.

"Want me to go with you?" Elizabeth called after us.

I stopped and turned back to my sister. Damon was standing beside her, his forehead creased with concern.

He's probably worried my dorkiness will rub off on him, I thought. After all—he'd touched me!

"No thanks. I'm fine. Really," I said.

Elizabeth hovered for a second.

"I'll go with her," Kristin told her. "Don't worry."

When we got into the ladies' room, Kristin started pulling big wads of paper towels out of the dispenser.

I went over to the sink and looked at myself. I watched my lower lip begin to tremble and a tear trickle down my cheek.

"Oh no." Kristin hurried over to me. "You are hurt, aren't you? What is it? Your knee?"

I shook my head and swallowed hard a couple of times. "No," I said when I could talk. "I'm not hurt. I'm just so embarrassed."

"Hey!" Kristin said brightly. "If it makes you

feel better, last year I wiped out in the middle of the cafeteria. Nobody let me forget that performance."

"But at least you didn't fall in front of Damon Ross. . . ." I broke off and buried my face in my hands. "I can't believe I did that!"

"Look, Jessica," Kristin said, kneeling down to blot at my pants. "If Damon is worth liking, he's not going to hold this against you. So, you fell in some sauce—it's no big deal."

I blew my nose, nodding and trying to believe what Kristin said.

Just then one of the bathroom-stall doors opened.

Kristin and I both jumped. I hadn't realized there was someone else in the bathroom.

I looked in the mirror. Lacey Frells's reflection smirked back at me.

Lacey walked over to the sink, eyeing me up and down. "Aren't you a little old for food fights, Jessica?"

"Knock it off, Lacey. Jessica fell pretty hard," Kristin said.

"So I just heard. For Damon Ross," Lacey purred, washing her hands and studying her perfectly cool reflection in the mirror.

I was mortified. For all I knew, Lacey would spread the word all over school that I liked

Damon. But I couldn't take any more of her nastiness. I had to say something.

"Isn't it kind of rude to eavesdrop on other people's conversations?" I snapped, hardly believing my own nerve.

Lacey pulled a towel out of the dispenser. "If you want to come in here and talk about your personal life, that's your problem. This is a *public* bathroom. *Public* as in *not private!* Get it?" Lacey wadded up her towel and tossed it into the waste can. Then she slunk out of the ladies' room. Shoulders slouched, sticking out her hips as she walked. Half rock star, half slithering snake.

I groaned. "Why does Lacey hate me so much?"

Kristin leaned against the sink. "She's probably mad I didn't tell her I was meeting you for lunch."

"Why didn't you tell her?" I asked.

"You're *my* friend, Jessica. I don't need *Lacey's* permission to hang out with you."

Silently Kristin and I stared at each other's reflections in the mirror.

I was thrilled Kristin wanted to be my friend. She was the sweetest cool person I had ever met. But Lacey certainly wasn't happy about it. And I had the feeling she was going to do everything in her power to sabotage our friendship.

Lacey and Kristin have been best friends forever, so I couldn't say anything to Kristin about it. I mean, if I turned against Lacey, Kristin would ditch me for sure.

Bending down, I finished wiping the sauce off my pants. For a few more seconds neither one of us said anything. Maybe I was being paranoid, but I couldn't wait to get out of there.

"Do you mind if we skip lunch?" I asked, not looking at Kristin. "I'm sorry, but I'm not hungry anymore. I think I just want to walk a little."

"You sure?" Kristin asked.

"Yeah. My leg feels kind of stiff. I should walk to make sure the muscle doesn't cramp up."

It was a lie. But I needed to get out in the fresh air and think.

"Okay." Kristin frowned. "But call me later?"

"Bye!" I said, and practically hurled myself out the door.

I didn't even look back at Damon's table to see if he was still there, watching me.

For the first time in my entire life, I wished I were invisible.

Lacey

Gel was playing with my lighter, turning the flame all the way up until it was practically burning his shiny nose off.

"So anyway, I shot six Krotop Warriors in, like, one and a half seconds. Just blew 'em off the screen. I think it was my personal best." He rubbed his hand over his face like he was exhausted from last night's video-game combat.

I rolled my eyes. Gel is always bragging about his video-game scores as if he's been fighting for real. Like he's some kind of war hero. It's kind of hilarious. I mean, Gel is *not* the toughest guy in the world. But I'm not into big football player types anyway.

I shot a look at Kristin to see how she was enjoying Gel's stimulating conversation. She nodded, doing a good job of acting like she actually cared.

The truth is, Kristin thinks Gel's a creep. And she was probably wishing he'd get lost so we could talk.

She'd come over to our booth about five minutes after our little scene in the bathroom. I'd seen Jessica leave, and now I didn't know if Kristin was going to blast me for chasing off her little friend or apologize for hanging out with Jessica when she knew I didn't like her.

Gel glanced out the window and gasped. Some little kids were leaning on his car, which was parked along the curb. "Back in five," he said shortly, sliding out of the booth and trying not to break into a run.

I stared outside, watching Gel as he shooed away the kids and made sure they hadn't left any fingerprints on his wax job.

I rolled a cigarette around on the table. Waiting.

When Kristin didn't say anything, I smashed the unlit cigarette into the soil of this little potted violet on our table and stared at the ceiling. "Well?" I said finally.

"What's your problem?" she asked.

"What do you think?" I responded, indignant.

"Okay," Kristin said. "Am I not supposed to like Jessica because *you* don't like Jessica?"

Jessica Wakefield. She seemed to be fouling up my life every time I turned around lately. I had to admit, I wasn't too happy about her and

23

Kristin hanging out. Kristin was supposed to be *my* friend.

"Hey, in case you forgot, Jessica got me into big trouble," I reminded Kristin. "It seems like you could show a little loyalty." I mean, I'd made a big effort for Jessica when she first came to our school. I'd talked to her, I'd asked her to skate with me in the park once, and I'd introduced her to some members of Splendora, this band I hang out with sometimes. Was it wrong of me to expect her to do something for me in return? Instead she'd told on me so I couldn't cut class to hang out with Gel—I thought that was pretty low.

"I just asked her for one little lie," I reminded Kristin. "All she had to do was tell the teacher I was part of the track team so I could leave class early. And did she do it? No."

"She couldn't," Kristin pointed out.

"Why? Because Bethel McCoy didn't approve?"

Bethel is this girl for whom track is, like, a religion. She made a stink about how I hadn't shown up for practice and wasn't on the team. Then Jessica caved in and backed off our little story. "Jessica Wakefield has no guts," I said. "I mean, who cares what Bethel thinks? Only geeks like Jessica, that's who."

Kristin crossed her arms and got this funny look on her face.

"What? What's that look?"

She pressed her lips together, like something was on her mind—and whatever it was wasn't pretty.

"What?" I said again. "Jessica Wakefield may be a gutless wonder. But I'm not. You've got a problem with me? Tell me. I can take it."

"This isn't about Jessica. It's like . . . you have a really warped sense of what people *owe you,* Lacey," Kristin blurted out.

"What people? Jessica?"

She stared at me. Not saying anything.

"You?"

Her eyes flickered.

"What?" I asked, exasperated.

"Well, for one thing, you're *always* asking to copy my homework," Kristin said.

I knew there was a long list of things Kristin could have brought up. I mean, what about all those times I'd ditched her to hang out with Gel or Splendora? It was pretty nice of her to only bring up the homework thing.

"But I don't have time to do homework," I explained defensively. "I've told you a million times. Between dating Gel and . . ." I trailed off when I saw Kristin's face. She was glaring at me.

Not a hateful glare, more like a *disappointed* glare.

I don't know how she manages to do it, but Kristin is the one person in the world who can make me feel totally ashamed of myself. "Okay. Okay. I'm sorry. What do you want from me?" I said, giving in.

"I want you to quit using me as your little homework slave," she said, raising her eyebrows.

"I don't—," I started, about to defend myself. But I broke off. I couldn't do it—Kristin just makes me feel too guilty. "Okay, okay! I'm *really* sorry!" I exclaimed, crossing my arms and looking her right in the eye. I was being dramatic, hoping to get a smile out of her.

But Kristin just pursed her lips and looked away. Like she didn't really believe my apology.

Gel came back and slid into the booth next to me. He took a sip of soda and banged his glass down on the tabletop. "Well! Got that taken care of," he said, like he'd just faced down a vicious gang of thugs or something. Really, he is such a moron sometimes.

I figured with Gel around, Kristin wouldn't stay for lunch—I was right.

"I gotta go," she said quickly. "Want to go to the mall later?"

It was her way of saying we were still cool. Unfortunately I couldn't take her up on the offer.

"Can't," I said. "I have to baby-sit." I couldn't ask Kristin to ruin her Saturday and come watch Penelope with me. Not now. She was mad enough at me already.

"Lucky you. Have fun," she said, and stood up.

"Ha, ha," I answered dryly.

Gel gave Kristin a tired wave. When she was gone, he put his head on my shoulder. "Lace, I want to tell you something."

I groaned and shoved him off my shoulder. "Sit up," I told him, wishing he'd left instead of Kristin. I hoped Kristin wasn't still mad at me.

Gel gave me a hurt look. "What's with you?"

"Nothing's with me," I muttered.

Gel let out this long, tragic sigh. "Lacey, I was going to try to do this nicely, but . . ."

I turned and stared at him. His brown eyes looked vaguely sad. "What are you talking about?" I demanded.

"I want to break up," he said. He shrugged— as if what he'd just said was no big deal.

I felt like somebody had socked me in the stomach. It took me a minute to recover. He was kidding. He had to be kidding.

Gel pushed back his notoriously gelled hair and gave me his sad-puppy-dog face. "I'm sort of . . ."

"Sort of what?" I demanded.

"I'm feeling, um, kind of boxed in. I need space. And . . . um, there's this girl at school I . . ."

"You're seeing somebody else?"

Gel tried to look like he was sorry about it. He was really playing this for tragedy. But he couldn't keep from smirking. "I didn't plan it," he said, his voice full of phony remorse.

If he was expecting me to start sobbing, he was going to be really disappointed.

Gel wasn't *that* good-looking. And I had a hard time believing he could date some chick in high school who would look better on his arm than I did. Any high-school chick who *was* better looking than me wouldn't give Gel the time of day.

This whole story was probably a big lie.

I decided to call his bluff. I lit a cigarette and rolled my eyes at him. "Well, if you think you can do better than me, go right ahead."

"Don't be like that," he whined, still trying to turn the conversation into a big drama. Obviously he wanted me to beg him not to leave.

In his dreams!

The waitress came over and put our pizza down on the table, leaving the check beside it.

"You can't smoke that in here, miss," she said before she left.

I tossed my cigarette in Gel's soda, put a napkin in my lap, and helped myself to a slice.

"Don't you have anything to say?" Gel asked, watching me eat.

I picked up the check and handed it to him. "Yeah. Pay this on the way out, would you?"

Gel sighed and slid out of the booth. I didn't even turn my head to look at him. I just kept on eating.

I flicked my eyes around the restaurant. The two girls at the table to my left weren't looking at me. But they weren't talking to each other either. They had probably heard the whole thing. Even my little fight with Kristin. They were probably just waiting for me to leave so they could start gabbing.

Well, let them wait. I wasn't going to rush out of there like I was all upset. Nobody was going to see me sweat.

A few minutes later I saw Gel on the sidewalk outside, climbing into his car. Just in case I wasn't watching, he pulled out fast enough to make his tires squeal so I'd have to notice him.

It was almost funny. Almost. But not really.

I figured Gel would last maybe twenty-four hours on his own. He might even work up the nerve to call some other girl. When he got the big turndown, he'd come running back.

And I'd take him back. But not right away.

I wanted to see *him* sweat.

I watched that Damon kid skip down the steps and head the opposite way than Gel had gone.

I had to hand it to Jessica, he *was* pretty hot for a football player type. In fact, now that I was technically single, I wouldn't mind flirting with Damon a little myself.

And if Gel didn't come around soon enough, wouldn't a new guy be the perfect thing to make him jealous?

Jessica

I never realized before I started running how exercise helps clear your head.

I've been running every Sunday since I joined the track team. Usually I just jog around the neighborhood, but if I'm feeling energetic, I do a five-mile loop around school and back. I was a little late today. I'd been waiting for Bethel to come jog with me, but she'd finally called and told me she felt like she was coming down with something, so I left without her.

I ran faster up the hill on Redwood. Coach Krebs said to use your hips going up hills, not to let your knees take all the beating. I focused on my hips.

I turned in front of school and sprinted down the grassy hill and across the playing field. When I came up on the other side and turned down Verde Street, I spotted a flash of white T-shirt jogging up the sidewalk about a block in front of me.

31

Okay, Wakefield, I said to myself. *Let's take them on!*

I increased my pace, trying to stay light on my feet as I closed the gap between me and the other runner. I could see now that it was a boy.

I leaned into it, trying to keep my breaths even and watching the flash of neon on the soles of the boy's running shoes. He was tall, and his stride was long. I didn't know if I could pass him or even keep up with him. He reached up and wiped his forehead, turning his head to the side. I caught a glimpse of his profile, and my heart flip-flopped.

It was Damon!

I dropped back to a slow jog, trailing him from a distance while he turned the corner and headed down Banks Lane.

I followed him to the end of Banks, around the corner, and down Hollis Avenue, where all the big, fancy houses are. I stayed far enough away that if Damon turned around, he wouldn't recognize me, but close enough so I wouldn't lose him.

Where was he headed, I wondered. Home?

As we ran along Hollis Avenue, I played a game with myself. I tried to see if I could match Damon with any of the houses we were passing.

I could definitely see him living in the sprawling, modern, split-level house down the street with no windows in the front. Maybe he was the son of some reclusive rich people. Artists. Somebody eccentric, who didn't want any attention. And maybe Damon was kind of eccentric too. And shy.

But Damon didn't stop in front of the modern house, and I started rethinking my theory. Maybe he lived in one of the restored brick mansions up ahead on the right and came from some really old family with a crest over the fireplace. And maybe he really was a snob.

We passed the big mansions, and I was relieved.

As I followed, I couldn't help noticing that Damon had a nice way of moving. He jogged from the hips like you were supposed to, and he kept his arms close to his sides.

We left Hollis Avenue and jogged down a few blocks where the homes were more modest. It was a pretty neighborhood, with lots of old-fashioned, gingerbread-type houses.

Yeah. I could see Damon as an old-fashioned, porch-swing kind of guy.

I kept waiting for him to slow down and go running up one of the walks.

Instead he began to run faster. Like he was

impatient to get where he was going.

I'd never run this far before. No wonder Damon looked like a football player. He must be in really good shape.

We left the gingerbread neighborhood and passed by Briggs Park.

Briggs Park is not the safest park in the world. In fact, the area south of Briggs Park, which is called Briggs Heights, is really kind of seedy. I'd driven through it a couple of times with my parents, but I'd never been there on foot. And I'd never even dreamed of going there alone. I didn't think it was safe.

The people looked normal and everything. Kids were playing in yards. People were out mowing their lawns. Stuff like that. But scattered between the houses were lots of trailers.

People always make jokes about trailers. About how only really poor, really messed-up people live in them. But when I got up close, most of them looked really nice. Like mini-homes. They had awnings. Porches. Little patio areas.

It didn't occur to me that Damon might actually live in a neighborhood like this. So I kept on jogging and came within twenty feet of Damon when he paused outside one of the trailers.

I stopped short and ducked behind an old, rusty car, praying he hadn't seen me.

The trailer was a little older than the others, but it looked okay. It had a crisp green-and-white-striped awning that stretched out over a little patio play area with a low fence around it.

Damon stood outside the fence for a moment, then he jumped over it, trotted up to the door, and let himself in.

I stood outside, blown away. No way could Damon live here. In a trailer? Come on! Maybe this wasn't his home. Maybe he was just visiting somebody.

Like a friend. Or—a girl?

I backed up and leaned against a big tree, where I could see the trailer without being seen.

Two minutes later he came back outside. With *two* girls. His little sisters.

I'd met them before. At the mall and at the movie theater. One was two and the other one was around four.

He lifted them both up and began to spin. They screamed and giggled.

"Damon!" A woman came out wearing a pink polyester dress with a white apron over it. She was obviously a waitress. "I'm leaving now. There's lasagna for dinner—just heat it up. Don't let the girls stay up too late. And don't spoil them," she added in a mock-stern voice.

"Yes, Mom," Damon said, bouncing the girls and making them laugh even more.

"And lock the door when you come and go."

"Yes, Mom," Damon said in a comic tone, as if they had been through this about a thousand times.

"And Damon . . ."

"Yes, Mom?"

"Take a shower," his mother said, laughing.

"What for?"

The older girl put her arms around Damon's legs and shouted loudly, "Because you stink!"

The younger girl tried to copy her sister, grabbing the knees of Damon's sweatpants and hopping up and down.

"I do not!" Damon protested, grabbing at both his sisters and tickling them.

Their mother laughed again. "But you're still the best son in the whole wide world—even if you smell."

Damon reached over to hug his mom. "And you're the best mom in the whole wide world. Know that?"

She ran a hand over his hair. "I know," she said, grinning. Her expression turned soft. "Thanks, Damon. I know you'd rather be out with your friends—"

"Gimme a break. Would you get out of here?" Damon pushed her away with a cocky smile.

"All right, all right." His mother turned and headed out the gate. "See you later. Have fun," she called. She walked over to a dented old station wagon and climbed in. It took the engine several tries to turn over, but finally it started, and Mrs. Ross drove down the potholed road that led downtown.

My heart was thundering in my chest.

I backed carefully away. Then, when I was sure I was out of sight, I broke into a run.

I felt bad. Really bad. I wished I hadn't followed him. Now I felt like a big snoop.

Damon Ross lived in a trailer. No wonder nobody knew anything about him. If my family were in the same situation, I probably wouldn't tell people either.

I didn't slow down till I got to the gingerbread neighborhood.

Okay. So Damon didn't live in a modern fortress, a big mansion, or a cute old house.

He lived in a trailer. So? He had to help his mom out with his sisters while she worked as a waitress in the kind of restaurant where people wore pink uniforms. So?

So—Damon was poor. He had to baby-sit because his mom couldn't afford a sitter—that's why he never hung out with anyone after school or played on any teams. He wasn't shy or snobby; he was *busy*.

Oh, and he was really sweet to his mom. And really cute with his sisters.

I felt terrible for spying on Damon. I'd *die* if he ever found out.

But now I couldn't help myself—I liked him even more.

A Page from Damon Ross's Journal

Sunday, October 11

Here we are again, alone together on a Sunday night.

Ugh!

Why is it I have no trouble writing in this stupid thing, but I never get around to doing my homework?

Can't blame it on the girls. They've been asleep since eight. They've been really good about bedtime lately. I don't get much argument. Probably because - the TV's still broken.

Man! I really miss it. <u>No football.</u> I don't have time to be on the team, but at least I could still watch some games before the set died. And the noise kept me company. I guess I'm all on my own now. It would be nice to have someone to hang out with. But that's stupid. I mean, who could resist an offer like, "Hey, want to come over to my mobile home and not watch TV?"

Stupid. But I can still dream about having someone over, can't I?

Specifically: Jessica Wakefield.

I really blew it yesterday. I am such an idiot. She must have been pretty embarrassed after that fall— and instead of helping her up, what do I do? I call more attention to her by telling her to lie there in a puddle of spaghetti sauce. No wonder she walked right by me and didn't say anything when she came back out of the bathroom. I saw her leave Vito's alone right after that. I hope she was all right.

I thought maybe Kristin Seltzer would come over and say something to me about it. But she didn't. She sat with Lacey Frells instead.

I don't usually hang out at Vito's—it's too much of a scene. The only reason I was even in there today was because I was hungry and I wanted to see Jessica.

Too bad I was such an idiot in front of her.

I've been watching her (great—now I'm a stalker, I guess), and there's something about Jessica that I really like. She's not afraid to be herself. I've even seen her stand up for herself a couple of times. She's brave.

I don't think Jessica's made that many friends yet, but at least she's trying to fit in and make new friends. I don't even try.

Friends mean too much explaining. Telling people why I can't do this and can't do that. About where I live. About my family. Not that I'm ashamed. I'm _not!_ But I guess I've just heard one too many comments about "trailer trash." And it makes me really mad. Especially since I know how hard Mom works.

It's better if I never have to tell anyone the truth. Still, I wonder what Jessica would think if she knew.

Lacey

Kristin answered the doorbell on the first ring. It was six o'clock on Sunday night, and I'd walked all the way to her apartment.

"What's wrong?" she asked the second she saw my face.

"Gel broke up with me," I said. "Can I come in?"

Kristin reached out and took my hand, pulling me inside. "Let's make some tea. You can tell me all about it."

Kristin makes awesome tea. It's herbal, but she puts all this extra stuff in it to make it taste really amazing. She won't tell what it is either. It's like her secret potion. And it really is calming. At least it calms *me* down.

"Drink." She put a mug in front of me and then got a big bag of double-chocolate cookies from the pantry.

"Now." She sat down with her own tea. "What happened?"

"Yesterday, after you left? He said he had some other girl."

"Why didn't you call me?"

"Because I didn't believe him. But then like an hour ago I saw him driving down the street, and there *was* a girl in his car. It was dark, so I couldn't see what she looked like. But it was definitely a girl."

Kristin took a sip and looked at me over the top of her mug. "Yeah, but how do you know it was his new girlfriend? She could've been his cousin or something."

I felt a tear slip down my cheek. Kristin grabbed a box of tissues off the kitchen counter and started patting me on the back. I took a tissue and blew my nose.

I couldn't help it. It wouldn't have bugged me too much if Gel and I had had a fight and he'd walked. Then I'd know he would come back. He *always* came back. But if he'd found someone else, he might actually be gone for good.

"You'll meet somebody else," Kristin said.

"Nobody in high school." I sniffled. "Nobody that has a *car*."

"Having a car isn't everything," she pointed out.

"Yeah, well, it *is* when you hate where you live and want to get as far away as possible as fast as possible."

Kristin's parents are divorced, like mine. But at least she lives with her mom.

"Are things still really bad at home?"

"The only time my stepmom ever talks to me is when she's asking me to baby-sit. She thinks she's such a big deal because she's an architect. Her time is important. My time is totally disposable."

"Can't you talk to your dad?"

"He just stays at the office so he doesn't have to listen to us complain about each other. Besides, he always sides with Victoria." I looked up at Kristin. "What am I going to do? Gel is all I've got. I have to get him back."

Kristin sat back down on her side of the table and shrugged. "I don't know. If you think Gel is all you've got, you're nuts." She smiled. "You've got brains. You've got looks. And you've got *me,*" she said in a perky voice.

I felt the knot in my stomach relax a tiny bit. Really and truly, I had been afraid that maybe Kristin was mad at me for yesterday. But she was still my best friend, which meant I was okay.

Minus my boyfriend. But okay.

I swallowed a sip of tea and smiled. "Thanks," I said. "You're right."

"To us. Best friends forever," Kristin said, clinking mugs with me. "Hey! You know what next Saturday is, don't you?"

"No!" I exclaimed, putting my mug down with a bang.

"Yes!" Kristin grinned. "It's our anniversary."

"I can't believe it. I almost forgot. I am soooo sorry. But I am soooo glad you reminded me."

Kristin and I always celebrate the day we met. It was in second grade, at our friend Sally's birthday party at Pirate's Ice Cream Cove. It's this totally corny ice-cream parlor that gives out eye patches if you order the Pirate's Treasure Chest Special—five scoops of ice cream, three kinds of sauce, nuts, sprinkles, candy bits, bananas, and cherries.

We were the only two kids at the party who ordered the Pirate's Treasure Chest Special and got the eye patches. Of course, we were also the only two kids at the party who threw up. But when you're in second grade, you don't care too much about that stuff.

Every year we go back on the same day, order the Pirate's Treasure Chest Special, and eat them wearing the eye patches. (We're always careful to make sure no one from school is around, though.)

Luckily we don't throw up anymore.

Kristin let out this silly giggle and put her hand over her eye like an eye patch. I sort of half sniffled, half snorted and put my hand over my eye too.

Suddenly things didn't look so bad.

"So it's a date?" Kristin asked.

"It's a definite date," I said. I glanced at the clock. "Oh no! Gotta split. It's that time again. Bleecchhh!"

"Baby-sitting?"

"Yeah. Dad and Victoria are going to have dinner with some new client of hers. So I'm stuck with Penelope all night." I shrugged. "At least I'm making cigarette money."

"You have to quit smoking, Lace," Kristin said as she walked me to the door and gave me a hug. "Hang in there. You'll be fine."

I squeezed Kristin back and started toward my house.

"Lacey! Is that you?" Victoria's voice held that subzero warmth that I'd come to know and love.

"No. It's the neighborhood ax murderer," I replied in a flat tone. I walked into the living room. Victoria sat on the black-and-white sofa, wearing a white wool suit with black patent-leather buttons.

Penelope sat in her lap, wearing little black-and-white overalls and holding a little black-and-white stuffed animal.

Victoria let out a big sigh—as if she thought I was just impossible. "Please don't say things like that in front of Penelope. *She* has an active

45

imagination. That's not the way I want it stimulated."

I loved the emphasis on *"she."* Like I was some kind of uncreative clod compared to Penelope. Victoria was always doing that. Making little digs at my taste in clothes, food, friends, music. Whatever.

"So I guess that means no horror movies tonight?" I asked.

She stood up with a pained look that told me she had decided to ignore my remark. "I'm on my way to pick up your father at the club. Then we'll be meeting the Johnsons. I left their number in the kitchen in case you need to reach us."

Victoria pointed to a pile of picture books on the coffee table. "Please. No television. No rock music. Just read to her. All right?"

"You got it," I said, dropping my purse in a chair.

Victoria stared at it for a moment. I guess she was debating whether or not to yell at me for cluttering up the living room with my stuff. My purse is electric blue. It totally clashed. She probably wouldn't have minded if it was black—or white.

Finally she decided not to say anything.

Victoria leaned over and gave Penelope a hug and a kiss. "See you later, sweetheart," she cooed. "Have a good evening," she told me in a curt tone.

I heard her high heels click along the black-and-white marble floor in the front hall. Then the front door clicked shut, and she was gone.

I threw myself on the sofa and glared at the stack of picture books. I hated it. I hated Victoria telling me what to do. She acted like I was some kind of hired nanny. She acted like she and Penelope were Dad's family and I was just some cranky *relative* they had to live with.

I picked up Penelope's picture-book version of Cinderella and glanced at the pages. "Don't worry about it, Cinderella, babe," I said to the pictures. "I know just how you feel."

Still, I was glad Victoria didn't pay that much attention to me. One good thing about a dad who's never home and a stepmom who doesn't like you is that they tend to ignore you. Unless they need me to baby-sit, they don't care where I am or what I'm doing. Which leaves me free to do—well, just about anything. As long as I'm home by ten-thirty, which is a pretty late curfew for an eighth-grader.

But without Gel I had nowhere to go and no way of getting there.

"Can we play a game?" Penelope asked me,

leaning over my shoulder to distract me from the book.

"How about hide-and-seek?" I suggested, shutting the book and tossing it aside. "You go hide, and I'll come find you."

"Okay!" she answered brightly.

"I'll close my eyes and count to ten." I closed my eyes. "One . . . two . . . three . . . four . . ."

I could hear her scurrying around, running up the stairs and into her mother's closet. Eventually she'd start playing with Victoria's clothes and forget all about hide-and-seek. Which would accomplish a double goal. One, I wouldn't have to entertain the little rug rat all night, and two, Victoria would come home to find out her precious Penelope had strewn her fabulous black-and-white wardrobe all over the place. Excellent.

When I got to ten, I lay down on the sofa, turned on the TV, and got down to thinking how I was going to use Damon Ross to get Gel back.

Gel was really a pretty jealous guy. If I acted like I didn't care that he'd dumped me and found a new, much better-looking man, Gel wouldn't be able to stand it. He'd come running back.

My new boyfriend had to be *so* fantastic

looking that it would drive Gel nuts. And that's where Damon came in.

The more I thought about it, the more I liked the idea. Not only would it make Gel insanely jealous, it would show that loser Jessica Wakefield that Damon has superior taste in girl-friends—me.

Jessica

"Phone!" Elizabeth called from her desk, where she was busily typing away at her computer.

It was Sunday night, and I'd already showered and picked out what I was going to wear to school the next day—my fuchsia tank top, my dark bootleg jeans with the little pink flowers embroidered on the hems, and my pink platform sandals.

I lay faceup on my bed, waiting for my nails to dry and thinking about Damon. Every time I remembered him swinging his little sisters around, I got dizzy. He was *so* cute!

"Jessica—it's Kristin," Elizabeth shouted.

I swung myself off the bed, hurried through the bathroom separating my twin's bedroom from mine, and snatched the receiver out of her hand.

"Thanks. Hello?" I said, dragging the phone back into my room.

"Hey, Jessica. How are you? Feeling better?"

"Yeah," I said, pleased that she sounded so concerned.

"I was thinking, you know, if you really like Damon—well, maybe I could help," Kristin offered. "I mean, I don't know him very well, but maybe I could hint around or something."

"Okay, but I don't want to make a big deal out of this," I said cautiously.

"Oh, I completely understand. I won't do anything unless it's really, really subtle."

"Thanks, Kristin," I said gratefully.

"Okay, I have to go. But plan A will begin tomorrow at oh-eight-hundred hours," she said, giggling. "Affirmative?"

"Affirmative." I laughed. "And I've found out a few things about our man of mystery—I'll tell you tomorrow."

"Tell me now!" Kristin said.

"Well, today when I—," I began.

"Oh, Jess, Mom's calling me. I really have to go."

"Don't worry. I'll tell you tomorrow," I said, disappointed that I couldn't finish.

"Okay. See you then," Kristin said.

"Bye."

I hung up, wondering how I was ever going to get to sleep.

*   *   *

When I saw Damon in the hall by our lockers first thing Monday morning, my hands started to sweat. *Are you really there, or am I imagining you?* I thought. *Do you know how sorry I am for spying on you? For finding out your secret?* When he got closer, my breath came in little gasps because my heart was beating so fast.

He was looking at me. Making eye contact. Smiling. He was *so* gorgeous.

"Hi!" he said. "How are you?"

I meant to say "hi" and "fine." But my tongue got all twisted up, and what came out was, "Hine!"

Hine?

What was my problem? I did my best to smile, picked up my bag, and scurried away like some kind of frightened squirrel.

Was I jinxed around this guy? Doomed to embarrass myself every time he looked my way?

And what was with his smile and the "hi"? Was it his way of saying, "Klutzes are people too, so don't worry if you're a dork"? Or his way of saying, "I'd like to get to know you"? But clearly he had no idea I'd followed him home on Sunday afternoon. And that was a good thing— a *very* good thing.

But I *was* going to need major help on the

Damon front if I was going to have any chance of making him think I wasn't a complete loser.

"So what's going on?" Kristin asked at lunchtime.

She raised her hand and waved at someone behind me.

I turned. It was Lacey, getting a soda out of the vending machine.

Lacey waved back and then held a hand over her eye.

Kristin broke out laughing. Lacey walked out of the cafeteria with her soda, a huge grin plastered on her face.

I turned back to Kristin. "What was that about?" I asked.

Kristin flapped her hand, like it was too silly to explain. "Inside joke," she said, still chuckling. "Now, tell me what's up?"

Suddenly I felt a little uncomfortable. I mean, Kristin isn't *my* best friend. She's *Lacey's* best friend.

But there Kristin was, sitting across from me with a big, friendly smile on her face.

"Well? What's up? What's the big news?" she asked again.

I hesitated. "Okay," I said finally. "I have

some information about our man of mystery."

"Damon?"

I nodded. "This is going to sound really weird, so you have to promise not to laugh. Okay?"

"I swear," Kristin said solemnly, and leaned forward to listen.

I took a deep breath and glanced around to make sure no one else was listening. "Okay. Yesterday I was out running, and when I passed the school, I saw Damon running way ahead of me. So, I followed him."

"Oh my God! What happened?" Kristin demanded, her eyes wide.

"Well, we were running for a really long time. It turns out he lives in Briggs Heights. In a . . . um . . . mobile home. His mom is a waitress, and he baby-sits while she's at work. His little sisters are so cute, and he's really good with them. I kind of got the feeling that his dad was . . . gone."

"*Wow,*" Kristin said. "That's totally tough. No wonder Damon's never around."

"Exactly," I said.

Kristin squeezed some lemon into her diet soda and grinned. "I can't believe you followed him, Jessica—you're crazy!"

I felt my cheeks turn red. "Well, I didn't plan it or anything. It just kind of happened."

Kristin shrugged. I guess she didn't think I was as much of a loser for following Damon as *I* thought I was.

"So, he's not a snobby rich kid. It sort of makes me like him even more. I think it's so cool when good-looking guys have a sensitive side," Kristin said, waggling her eyebrows. "Don't you?"

"Yes," I said, and giggled with relief. "Really."

My old friends at Sweet Valley Middle School would think living in a trailer was just the creepiest thing they'd ever heard of. They'd think I'd really sunk to an all-time low, liking a guy whose family was . . . different.

But Kristin was smiling and giggling like she thought my crush on Damon was just the greatest.

"Do me a favor, will you?" I asked.

"Sure."

"Don't tell anyone about this. Not even Lacey." I didn't think Damon would want people to know. And I certainly didn't want the world to know I was creeping around, following boys I had crushes on. I mean, how lame can you get?

"Don't worry. It'll be our secret," Kristin promised. "No one else will know a thing."

Lacey Frells
English Composition

__Assignment:__ Write a paragraph starting with the phrase, "After high school . . ."

~~After high school I'm going to pack a suitcase full of my favorite clothes (all bright colors!) and go to college in a big city like New York and never come back to Sweet Valley. Ever. And, of course, I'll have my own car.~~

Six Reasons Why Gel Is a Loser

1. He always steals my cigarettes.
2. His car is gross.
3. His breath stinks.
4. His hair is all sticky.
5. He actually likes Jim Squalor.
6. I deserve better.

Lacey

I sat in study hall with my candy and soda, scribbling in my English composition notebook.

I'd finished my history and math homework over the weekend (part of my promise to not ask Kristin for her homework anymore). But I hadn't gotten to my English assignment. It was just a notebook exercise, not a hand-in assignment, but I thought I should do it anyway. Just in case the teacher asked us to read them out loud or something lame like that.

Whatever.

Sheila Watson sat down in the chair next to me, and I slammed my notebook closed. "Oh, Lacey," she whispered. "I heard you and Gel broke up, and I am soooooo sorry." Her voice was full of fake sympathy.

Sheila was a victim of rezoning and was new at school. She was trying to make her mark as the class gossip, and I had to admit she had a talent for it. She was perfectly annoying.

I stared at her. "Where'd you hear that?"

Sheila acted startled. "I don't know. From a lot of people. Everybody's talking about it. Was it some kind of secret?"

I bit my lip. No way had Kristin blabbed. So either the girls who had been at the next table had spread the word, or else Gel was bragging about dumping me at the high school and the story had circulated back to SVJH via somebody's younger brother or sister.

I glanced up and saw Ginger Walters and Mary Stillwater, two girls from the track team, over by the reference-book desk. They were whispering and sneaking looks in my direction.

They turned away when I caught their gaze.

"Are you devastated?" Sheila whispered. "I would be."

I was so annoyed, I actually stopped glaring at the track girls. "Look, Sheila," I snapped. "I make it a practice not to discuss my love life with somebody who's never had one."

Her mousy little face turned bright red. "Well, never mind, then. I was just trying to . . ." She practically fell over, she was in such a hurry to escape.

I shut my notebook and stood up. Suddenly the library felt a little too crowded. Maybe I'd go back to the cafeteria and talk to Kristin for a while.

I stalked down the hall. This thing with Gel was getting out of hand. No way was I going to have people expecting me to sob on their shoulder at the mention of his name.

There was no question. It was absolutely imperative now that I make Gel and everyone else believe I'd snagged Damon Ross.

So what if he'd totally ignored me every time I smiled at him today? I hadn't really been trying.

And now I would.

I had to figure out a way to get him to notice me.

Just one little glance was all I needed.

On my way back to the cafeteria I ran into Kristin coming out. "You're leaving? But you've got another ten minutes."

"I need to get my books," she explained.

"I'll walk to your locker with you," I said, falling in step beside her. "I've figured out how to handle the Gel thing."

"Oh yeah?"

The halls were starting to get crowded. Anna Wang and Salvador del Valle passed us. *Uh-oh. Jessica alert!* I thought, spotting the bland, blond person walking behind them.

But it wasn't Jessica. It was the even nerdier twin sister, Elizabeth. Still, I had to keep my voice down so the whole world wouldn't hear.

"Yeah, so listen. Gel's a total jealousy freak. If he thinks someone else wants me, he'll come running back. So I'm going after Damon Ross."

Kristin laughed.

I was totally offended. "What is so funny?" I demanded.

She shook her head, like she couldn't answer.

I flipped my hair off my shoulders. "Well, if that's how you're going to be, *fine*." I turned to walk away.

"Lacey! Lacey!" Kristin ran after me.

"I don't appreciate being laughed at," I said. "Especially not by my best friend."

She pulled me into an empty classroom and looked outside to make sure nobody was hanging around the door. Then she turned back to me. "I wasn't laughing at you," she insisted.

"Then why *were* you laughing?"

She chewed her lip. "If I tell you, you can't tell anybody else."

"Tell me what?"

"Look. It's just that Damon Ross is the *last* person in the world you would want to date."

"Why?" I demanded.

"Guess who has two little sisters and spends

most of his free time baby-sitting—which is, may I remind you, hardly your *favorite* activity in the whole world?"

"You're kidding," I said.

"Nope. Damon is in constant baby-sitters' hell. Jessica found out."

"Jessica? How?" I wanted to know.

Jessica, Jessica, Jessica. I also wanted to know why Kristin *insisted* on spending so much time with that *loser*. But I didn't ask.

Kristin grabbed my arm and narrowed her eyes.

"Ow, you're hurting me," I said, pulling away.

"Sorry," Kristin said. "Listen. Jessica made me promise not to tell anyone this, but Damon's probably not the best bet for you, Lacey. First of all, he lives in a mobile home in Briggs Heights. Second of all, he has absolutely no time since his dad seems to be out of the picture and his mom works. Damon has to baby-sit every day." She took a deep breath. "So, you wouldn't exactly be a match made in heaven." She paused. "But it's a secret, okay? I don't think Damon would want everyone in the world to know about his family situation, so don't spread it around. Got it?"

"*Okay,*" I said, processing. "And how, may I ask, did little Miss Jessica Wakefield get this juicy scoop on lover boy?"

"She followed him. She was jogging, and Damon was jogging ahead of her. So she followed him home." Kristin smiled, as if she thought that was cute or something.

I was totally awestruck. "And she actually *bragged* to you about this? Like she thought it was *cool?*" I asked. *"What a loser!"*

Kristin's brow clouded over. "Lacey, I told you all this to warn you off Damon, not to start something between you and Jessica. Okay?"

I wanted to say something to the effect that it would serve Jessica right for me to steal her crush and to tell the whole world that she was a stalking *freak*. But I held back. I knew it would only make Kristin mad if I started ragging on Jessica again.

Anyway. Thank God Kristin can't keep a secret from me to save her life.

"I'm glad you told me," I said with a straight face. "Poor guy."

"Hey!" Kristin opened her eyes real wide, like she was having a brilliant idea. "Maybe you and Damon could baby-sit *together*. I mean, seeing how much you *enjoy* children and baby-sitting, it would be a *perfect* date."

I could tell she was trying to change the tone of our whole little conversation. I cracked a smile. "You are such a comedian," I said.

The bell rang.

Kristin grinned cheesily. "Do yourself a favor, Lace. Forget about Damon. And just think . . . five scoops of ice cream. Three sauces. Pecans. Peanuts. Cherries. Once you eat that, all your troubles will just melt away."

"Until I get on the scale the next day."

"Stop that. No weight obsessing allowed."

"You're right. Anybody caught weight obsessing forfeits the eye patch."

"Good rule," Kristin said.

"Um, listen," I said, glancing at the notebooks in her arms. "I know this is a touchy subject with you, but . . ."

The smile left Kristin's face. "Lacey! I told you, I can't keep doing this for you."

"I know. I know," I said. "But I was so upset all weekend about Gel and . . ." I trailed off, letting her figure out the rest. I had promised I wouldn't ask her anymore. But I hoped she might let me get away with it one more time.

"Which homework are we talking about?" she asked.

"Math."

She chewed on her lip for a minute. Then she sighed and reached into her backpack, pulling out her notebook. "Don't copy it exactly," she instructed. "Get a couple wrong. Okay?"

"You got it," I promised.

"And this is the last time," she said. "I mean it."

"This is the last time I'll ask," I swore.

"Okay. Gotta go. See you later." Kristin hurried away, and I wandered down the hall with her math notebook.

The thing is, I'd already done the math.

I know, I'm twisted.

But I had to make sure. Kristin was still my best friend forever. No matter what.

Because I was really starting to wonder.

Kristin could keep all of Jessica's little secrets if she wanted, but I was still going for Damon Ross. Baby-sitting or no baby-sitting. That wasn't the point. I was going to make Gel *and* Jessica so jealous, they'd both turn green.

My brain was working overtime. Damon didn't have to baby-sit *all* the time. I saw him around Vito's occasionally. And I'd seen him around the mall after school. So I knew he had some free time. No reason why he shouldn't spend it with me.

I went to my locker to get out my math notebook. My purse fell out, and one of Penelope's little squeaky rubber bunnies rolled onto the floor. I grabbed my purse and hunted around, pushing aside my makeup case and a wad of old receipts. I knew there was a squeaky ladybug in there somewhere too. Sometimes Penelope's squeaky-toy fetish can be totally annoying. But today I was supremely grateful.

The bell was about to ring, so I had to hurry. I found the ladybug and put the two toys in the side pocket of my backpack. I'd never seen Damon in the cafeteria. But I'd seen him eating lunch by himself outside on the front steps a couple of times. Maybe it was his regular spot.

I looked out the front entrance. Bingo. There he was. Sitting on the steps, reading and eating a sandwich.

I went outside and sat down a couple of steps above him. I pulled my backpack in front of me and began rummaging around inside like I was trying to find something. Then I "accidentally" let the bunny and the ladybug fall out.

They made little squeaking sounds as they tumbled down the steps.

Damon looked up at me. Then he dropped his book and lunged forward to catch the toys. He actually got up and chased after the ladybug!

I groaned like this was the absolute last straw. "I am so sorry," I said. "I don't know if you ever have to baby-sit, but . . . I don't know what's worse, the kid or the booby traps. She puts this stuff in my backpack, and it drives me nuts!"

He tossed the toys back to me. "Yeah, I know," he said. "I usually get half-eaten cookies left in my backpack, which means I wind up having to clean out an inch of crumbs a week."

I gave him "The Smile."

He smiled back.

"So, how much baby-sitting do you get sentenced to?" I asked.

He laughed. "A *lot*."

"Yikes!"

"What about you?" he asked.

I rolled my eyes. "As little as I can get away with. When you're baby-sitting, an afternoon can seem like a week, you know?" Misery loves company. I wanted him to know I was just as miserable as he was.

He didn't say anything.

"Don't you think?" I pressed.

"It can be tiring," he said.

"My stepmother, who is always *so* busy, threatens to pull my allowance if I don't fall into line. It really makes me wonder why they call it an allowance—since I have to earn it," I added.

He looked a little uncomfortable.

"You get *paid*, don't you?" I asked.

"Oh yeah. Sure. But, uhhh . . . I don't really mind doing it. My sisters are pretty good kids."

He looked down at his sneakers, as if he didn't want to talk about it anymore.

Uh-oh! Maybe I had the wrong slant on this. Maybe he *liked* baby-sitting. In which case I was coming off like Snow White's stepmother.

I laughed—this really light ha-ha-ha-ha-ha-don't-mind-me kind of laugh. "I don't know why I act like I don't enjoy it. My little sister is really sweet. I'm kind of glad *my dad isn't around much either*—it gives me more time to spend with her."

Was it working? I wondered. Was he starting to get the feeling I was in the same boat as him?

He looked up. "How old?"

"My dad?" I asked, pretending to be confused.

Damon laughed. "Your sister," he corrected me.

"Oh. Three," I said, beaming as if Penelope were the sunshine of my life.

I prayed Damon hadn't seen me that time at the Red Bird Mall when some guys took Penelope's white stuffed bunny away from her. Jessica Wakefield—loser that she is—went chasing after them while I just sat there, watching. Damon finally fished the bunny out of this blue fountain (the water even turned the bunny blue) and gave it back to Jessica. I don't think he realized that it was actually *my* little sister's bunny

67

and I hadn't even *tried* to save it. Thank God."

Damon smiled. "I've got two sisters. Sally's four and a half. Kaia just turned two."

"Did you have a big birthday party for her?"

He smiled and shrugged. "I think she had fun."

"Penelope's birthday is coming up in a couple of weeks. I've been racking my brains trying to figure out what to get her."

It was all a total lie. Penelope's birthday was months away. And I couldn't have cared less about her present.

But Damon looked very interested. His big blue eyes were bright, and his gorgeous face was all enthused.

"There's this specialty toy shop in the mall," he said. "Toy Joy. Have you been there?" he asked, flicking his hair out of his eyes.

He really was breathtakingly hot. And I really was enjoying myself.

"No! But it sounds like fun. What are you doing this afternoon? Maybe you could show me. Help me pick something out."

He looked totally taken aback.

I stared into his eyes. I saw his throat tighten. He licked his lips. Would he go for it? Would he take the bait?

Yes, Damon. Lacey Frells is expressing interest in you. Don't panic. Be a man.

After a long pause he nodded and gave me a weak smile. "Yeah. Sure. I've got a couple of things I need to do. But I could meet you at the mall at four. Want to do that?"

"I would *love* to do that," I said in my throatiest voice. "See you at four. Just inside the front entrance."

"See you then," he agreed.

I stood up, waved, and walked back into the building. Sheila Watson was hanging out near the door. "Your fly is down," I told her, even though it wasn't.

Behind me, I heard her let out an embarrassed little squeal. I knew she'd probably come to a dead stop and look down at her fly, which of course makes you look like an idiot.

Honestly, some people are just too easy to fool.

Damon

"Oh, wow! Look at this!" Lacey picked up a hand puppet that had thick glasses and a big thatch of red hair. "If x is z and y is l, then how much is j if there are three people on a train to Cleveland and they don't serve lunch?"

I laughed. She'd just done a very good impression of our seventh-grade algebra teacher.

She tossed the puppet back into the bin with a sarcastic smile.

I followed her along an aisle, trying to figure out what had happened. One minute I'd been sitting on the steps eating a sandwich, and now here I was at the mall with Lacey Frells.

It wasn't that I didn't like her. In fact, she seemed kind of nice. It's just that I didn't really know her. And I was sure she didn't know anything about me. So why did she want me to be here? I mean, why didn't she just go shopping with her boyfriend?

"Look at this!" She pointed to an elaborate miniature hockey game. It had players, nets, goals. Everything. I mean, it was way cool.

"When it's activated, the players move around on a track and execute real plays. Sometimes I stop in here just to look at it," I admitted.

"Really?"

I nodded. I didn't say that the game was about as close to a real hockey game as I could get right now.

"There is definitely some cool stuff here," she agreed.

Even though Toy Joy is a toy store, the things in it are so awesome, you could spend hours in there no matter what age you are, just playing with stuff.

She watched the hockey players. "Hmmm. This might be a good gift for my dad. But not for a three-year-old girl. What did you get Sally when she turned three?"

"Hard to remember," I answered. "Look. Giraffes!" I veered toward a pair of giant stuffed giraffes, hoping to keep Lacey from asking me any more questions. So far I'd managed to dodge the ones I didn't want to answer. Or else I'd managed to finesse an answer without lying. Like the question of what I bought Sally? The answer was, not much.

And the one about getting paid to baby-sit?

My mom never paid me—except in gratitude.

"Those things are huge!" she whispered. "Do you think you could fit one in one of your sisters' rooms?"

I pictured the tiny cubicle of the trailer that was technically "the girls' room."

"No way," I answered truthfully. "How about you?"

"Maybe. The ceilings of our house are pretty high." She looked at the price tag. "But I'm not in the market for a twenty-five-hundred-dollar toy."

"Darn!" I said. "I was sort of hoping you'd buy two. They'd look so good together."

We laughed and moved on.

"Let's look at dolls," she suggested. "Do your sisters like dolls?"

"They love them," I said.

"What kinds?"

I wasn't really up on all the doll names. We picked up most of the dolls in thrift shops and garage sales. The boxes and labels were usually long gone.

"Like these?" Lacey led me over to a row of baby dolls in fancy boxes.

"Some. Yeah." I didn't mention that the baby dolls my sisters had were usually missing most of their hair—and sometimes an eye or a limb.

The things that really seemed to stand up to wear and tear were stuffed toys. You could find lots of those that were in pretty good shape at garage sales. "What about a teddy bear?" I suggested.

"Bears are good," she agreed. "Let's go look."

We headed for Bear Corner, where they had four gazillion stuffed bears. Big bears. Little bears. Bears in different colors. So many bears, it could drive you nuts.

Lacey reached into this huge pile of bears and pulled out one that was bright orange—wearing neon-colored patchwork overalls. "What do you think?" she asked me.

"It's—um . . . *colorful*," I said. *Kind of bizarrely colorful,* I thought. So colorful, it kind of hurt my eyes. But what did I know?

Lacey examined the bear with one eyebrow raised. Her mouth curved into a smile. "Yep. This is a very colorful bear, and my sister *loves* bright colors. I think this is the one. Come on. I'll pay for it, and then let's go get a soda or something."

I did a quick review of my financial situation. I figured I had enough for a drink. But that was about it.

I followed her to the cash register, where the clerk rang up the bear. Penelope was a lucky little girl to have a sister who cared enough about her to pick out just the right present.

It made me feel kind of like a slacker. I have to admit, I didn't put as much thought into choosing my sisters' toys.

The way I made toy runs was to hit the thrift shop, grab the first six things I could (*a*) afford and (*b*) carry, and then get out as soon as possible before I got tempted to buy stuff we didn't need and didn't have room for.

One thing about living in a trailer—before you buy even a magazine, you ask yourself, Now, where am I going to put this? And if the answer is, I don't know, you don't buy it.

Back out in the main hall of the mall, I followed Lacey as she strolled around, stopping in front of shop windows.

I couldn't help checking the place out to see if Jessica was here. I knew that Lacey and Kristin Seltzer were friends. And that Kristin and Jessica were friends. But I couldn't tell if Lacey and Jessica were friends. Lacey had mentioned Kristin a couple of times. But never Jessica.

"Let's go into here and play with the toys for grown-ups," Lacey suggested.

I followed her into Look Sharp. She was right—it was a toy store. Full of big, expensive toys for big kids.

"Hey. How do I look?" Lacey climbed up on a stationary bike that was designed to look like a big motorcycle.

I chuckled. "Pretty good."

"Too bad it can't take me anywhere." She climbed off. "What about that?" She pointed to an enormous, flat-screen TV.

"That is cool," I agreed. Man! Would I love a TV like that. Or *any* TV, really.

"This is what I need," she said, picking up a little bitty mobile phone.

Now there was something I could fit into my lifestyle. It wasn't much bigger than a computer mouse. I could put it right in my pocket.

The only thing was—I didn't have anybody to call. Or at least not up until now. Lacey was making it pretty clear she wanted to be friends.

Was I up to it? Maybe. If it didn't involve too much time or too many explanations.

Lacey

I had to literally drag Damon out of Look Sharp. I mean, it's sort of cool for five minutes, but I was sick of talking about toys and gadgets. I wanted to talk about *us*.

I led him into Lots o' Latte. It's a little café with tables outside the shop. Like an outdoor sidewalk café, indoors and minus the sidewalk.

It's a good place to be seen.

"So," I said after we got our drinks and sat down. "Tell me *your* theory about Miss Scarlett. Think she's an escapee from a mental asylum?" I figured gym class was a good place to start.

He laughed. "Nah. She just has an underdeveloped understanding of teenagers and an overdeveloped sense of smell."

I laughed, for real.

Miss Scarlett *is*, like, the weirdest PE teacher—*ever*. She's completely clueless and paranoid that you might forget to take your gym clothes home and wash them. That was the ultimate sin. She said it was a *"breeding ground for*

76

bacteria." I forge sick notes for gym *whenever* possible.

"This one time," Damon went on, "Miss Scarlett made us all show her our tongues. We were supposed to play basketball, but she went off on this complete tangent about good nutrition and the color of your tongue. Everyone started talking with their tongues hanging out of their mouths, like this—"

Damon stuck out his tongue and tried to say, "Hello, Lacey. Do I sound dumb?" but it came out like, "Hewo, Wafey. Poo—"

I almost spit. I was cracking up!! If some other guy had pulled the same stunt, it would have made me sick. But Damon was so cute, it just made him irresistible.

"I hope you don't get stuck like that." I giggled. "It might scare away the dates."

He made this ridiculous face—his tongue way out, his eyes really wide. I snorted and almost choked on a big gulp of soda. Then he looked at his watch, and his face went back to normal. Well, if you can call crazy-gorgeous normal.

"Yikes," he said. "I gotta get home."

"Time to watch your sisters?"

"You got it."

Damon picked up my shopping bag with

Penelope's Day-Glo bear in it, and we wandered toward the mall exit.

It was hot outside. I practically swooned when Damon kind of patted my shoulder and looked down into my eyes.

"I had a good time, Lacey," he said.

I don't know whether the hot air was doing tricks with my brain, but he was kind of stooping over me. Like he was thinking about giving me a hug or something. Poor guy, he spent so much time with little girls, he didn't know what to do with a grown one.

"Who would have thought," I said, smiling up at Damon's perfect face. "We'll have to try it again sometime soon. Okay?"

"Okay." He straightened up. "Well, see you tomorrow," he said. He handed me my shopping bag. "Hope Penelope likes the bear!"

"She'll love it," Lacey said. "And if she doesn't, then I'll keep it and get her something else. Because *I* love it."

We both laughed. Then I waved, and we headed out in opposite directions.

I was in such a good mood, I didn't even mind taking the bus home.

Jessica

"Got a couple of minutes?" I asked, poking my head into Elizabeth's room.

Elizabeth glanced up from her computer and then back to the screen, ignoring me. It was Monday night. Dinner was over, and I'd spent the last hour in my room, staring at my homework. But it was impossible. All I could think about was Damon Ross.

"Are we really talking a few minutes?" Elizabeth sighed, tapping her keyboard and not looking at me. "Or is that a code for 'hour and a half, minimum'?"

When I didn't answer, she stopped typing and swiveled around in her chair. "Uh-oh! Jessica-in-crisis alert!" She switched off her monitor. "Okay. What's up?"

I went into Elizabeth's room, closed the door, and threw myself on her bed with a big dramatic groan.

"That doesn't answer my question," Elizabeth said.

I flopped over on my back and let out an even bigger groan.

"Oh! Now I'm beginning to get it."

"Arggghhhhh!" I screamed.

"Is this about a boy?"

I sat up. "Damon Ross," I whispered at her.

"Whoa," Elizabeth whispered back.

"I like him."

She nodded. "Well, you have good taste."

"Here's the scary part—I *think* he might like me. But I can't really tell."

Elizabeth's eyes opened really wide. "All right. Now you have my attention." She came over and sat down cross-legged on the bed. "Go."

I settled back against her pillows and stared at the ceiling.

"Remember in Vito's, when I fell and he helped me up and everything?" I asked.

Elizabeth nodded.

"Well, I was so embarrassed. But that was really sweet of him, wasn't it?"

Elizabeth nodded again.

"Okay. And then today he said hello to me. I mean, what do you think that was about?" I asked.

Elizabeth looked at me as if I was IQ challenged. "Um, he just wanted to say hi?" she suggested in a kind, patient voice.

I sat up and scowled. "Listen. I can get all the sarcasm I want at school. I need help here!"

Elizabeth giggled. "I'm sorry. I guess I don't really know what to say. Damon worked on the paper when I was on the staff. He seemed really smart, but he was pretty quiet. That's all I know about him."

"Well, Kristin said maybe he's just a big snob. But that's not it at all," I said, taking a deep breath. "He lives in Briggs Heights."

I didn't say anything more. I wanted to see what Elizabeth's reaction would be.

Her reaction was *no* reaction. "So?"

"It's not that great a neighborhood."

She shrugged. "Remember Sophia from Sweet Valley Middle School? She lived in Briggs Heights before her mom married Mr. Thomas."

"And her brother was a total loser. A juvenile delinquent," I pointed out.

"So what are you telling me? That you like Damon? Or that you don't like Damon because he lives in Briggs Heights?"

"His family lives in a *trailer*," I said, watching her face closely.

Elizabeth's eyebrows went up.

"But he's not a wrong-side-of-the-tracks kind of guy at all," I blurted out quickly.

"I never said he was."

"I know. But some people might think that."

"I'm not some people."

"I know. I know. And it's sort of touching, really. I could see how hard his mom works—I think she's a waitress—and how much his sisters love him, and how he's got this really big sense of responsibility. I don't think his dad's around, so Damon is like the only man in the family. He's so sweet. And there are just a lot of people who would look at the trailer and never see anything else."

Elizabeth cocked her head. "How did you find out all this? Did he tell you?"

"Oh no." I shook my head. "Um . . . I kind of followed him."

Her face registered major shock. "Jessica! I cannot believe you did that," she gasped. "You spied on him?"

"I know." I started fidgeting with a loose thread on her bedspread. "I can't believe I did it either."

Elizabeth got up and went over to her desk again. She sat in her swivel chair and twirled around once before facing me.

"You know what I think?" she asked. "It's not me that you're trying to convince about Damon. You're trying to convince yourself. The question isn't what do *I* think about Damon Ross living in a trailer. The question is, what do *you* think about it."

"I think he's a great guy. And I don't care," I said.

I realized that what I'd said was true. I really didn't care *where* Damon lived.

All I wanted was for him to like me and for me to like him back. It was that simple.

Tomorrow I was going to look Damon right in the eye and smile.

And if he asked me how I was, I was going to say, "Fine," with an *F*.

Lacey

"What is that?" Victoria demanded when she came into the kitchen with Penelope on Tuesday morning. She froze when she saw the psychedelic bear sitting at the black-and-white breakfast table. The bear looked even more hideously garish in the kitchen light than it had in the store.

"It's for Penelope," I said.

Penelope let out this delighted squeal and ran toward it. "For me?" She grabbed it and hugged it. Poor kid. I guess she was starved for some color.

Two points for big sister. And another two points for the wicked stepdaughter.

Victoria was really irritated. I could tell. She was looking at the bear like it was a tarantula or something. I tried not to smile. All of Penelope's toys were black and white. Victoria had some theory about "positive/negative spatial relationships" and was counting on it to turn Penelope into a creative genius, just like her mother.

84

"What prompted this?" she asked.

I shrugged. "I just saw it and thought Penelope might enjoy something bright and cheerful."

I had her. She couldn't exactly yell at me for buying her kid a present. On the other hand, she knew that I knew what her tastes were. The bear didn't fit into the positive/negative stimulus category.

Victoria went over to the refrigerator and started taking out juice and milk. I could hear her muttering something under her breath about "passive aggression."

I left the kitchen without saying anything, got my books, and walked out the front door.

It was a nice day. Sunny and bright.

If I hadn't had to walk, I might have been in a good mood. Gel always picked me up and dropped me off in front of school. It wasn't a long walk, but I wasn't used to it. And now that people knew Gel and I had broken up, there was sort of a pride thing at stake.

"Hey, Lacey," Justin Campbell said as I walked up the school steps. "What happened to your boyfriend?"

I didn't answer, but as I walked by him, I managed to shoulder him—hard—and knock the books out of his arms.

His buddy, Matt Springmeier, let out this big laugh. "Whoa! She shot you down, man!"

Justin and Matt are pretty cool—I hang out with them sometimes. But like most guys, they have a jerky side. You can't let them win. Ever. If you do, they'll make your life miserable.

I walked in the front door and headed to my locker. Kristin and Jessica were standing across the hall by Kristin's locker, talking and laughing like best friends.

I opened my locker, took out a little rubber duck, and squeaked it until Kristin turned around.

"Is Penelope still putting those things in your backpack?" Kristin called with a laugh.

I smiled and sauntered over to her. "Yes. And it's the best thing she ever did. Because that's how I managed to meet *Damon Ross*. And guess what? We even went out. Yesterday we spent all day after school together."

Jessica's face turned a sickly gray. It was delicious.

Kristin's face froze.

I smiled at Jessica. "And it's all thanks to you."

"M-Me? What do you mean?" Jessica looked like she might burst into tears any minute.

"You're the one who told Kristin all about

Damon. I mean, following him is probably the *lamest* thing you've done to date. But knowing that he has to baby-sit his sisters really gave Damon and me something in common. So I started talking to him, and the rest is history."

Jessica's shocked gaze had shifted away from me. Now she was staring at Kristin with narrow eyes.

"You told?" Jessica cried. "But you promised!"

"I'm sorry," Kristin spluttered. "I was trying to help. . . . I know Lacey *hates* to baby-sit . . . and I thought there was no way . . ."

Jessica was glaring at Kristin.

And Kristin was glaring at me.

Jessica stomped off.

Kristin shook her head, her hands on her hips, still staring at me.

Then she took off too.

I went back to my locker to get my books.

Jessica Lamefield had actually believed that Kristin wouldn't tell me everything?

What was she thinking?

I didn't like having Kristin mad at me. But I didn't like how cushy she was getting with Jessica either. And from what I could judge, I had just taken care of that little problem.

Once Kristin cooled down, I'd apologize.

She'd get over it. She had to. She was my best friend.

Brian Rainey and Peter Glosser came over to Peter's locker, which is next to mine.

"Check it out—Jim Squalor is going to be at the mall!" Brian said to Peter. He was waving a flyer.

"No way! For real?"

"Yeah. I wonder what he looks like."

Peter laughed. "Think he'll do the Squalor Holler?"

Both guys made this really revolting noise that sounded like somebody hocking up a huge hunk of phlegm—imitating Jim Squalor.

I rolled my eyes and walked on down the hall. Gel tried to imitate the Squalor Holler all the time. It really got on my nerves. Jim Squalor was Gel's favorite DJ. A lot of people thought he was cool. Guys especially. *Normal* people found him revolting.

Roger Milton was taping the Jim Squalor flyers up on people's lockers.

"If you want to see Squalor up close, better get there early," he told me. "Half the town's going to be there."

My brain started cranking. Gel loved Jim Squalor. No way would he miss a chance to meet his hero.

All I had to do was set another mall date with Damon, make sure we were in the mall at the right time and the right place—and Gel would have to see us.

His jealousy buttons would be popping in nine different directions.

Sometimes I'm such a genius, I scare myself.

After second period I spotted Damon down by the water fountain.

"Damon!" I shouted.

Damon looked up and smiled, wiping water off his mouth. "Hey!" He came over and fell into step beside me.

"Interested in another mall run?"

"Uh . . . sure. If I can. When?"

"Saturday?"

"Mmmm—okay. If it's early. I have to be home by around one-thirty. What are we doing? Toy shopping again?"

I shook my head. "Nope. Jim Squalor's going to be at the mall, and I really want to see him."

Damon gave me an are-you-serious? look and started laughing. "Sorry," he said when he got his breath back. "Somehow you don't strike me as a big Jim Squalor fan."

"I'm not really, but I'm curious. He's so gross.

It'll be like watching a car wreck. Come on, admit it. You want to check him out too."

He thought it over. "Okay. Sure. I guess I'm as curious as the next person. Count me in."

"All right, then." I gave him my sexiest stare. "It's a date."

JIM SQUALOR FLYER

102.6 FM WSVAL presents ...

Jim Squalor LIVE!!

Outrageous DJ and man o' music,
with wisecracks so sharp they'll make you bleed.

SWEET VALLEY MALL

Saturday, October 17, 11:30 A.M.–3:00 P.M.

Promoting ...

BIG ELECTRO CUTIEPIES

BIG PALM PARK STADIUM

SATURDAY, OCTOBER 17, 8 P.M.

TICKETS ON SALE AT A RECORD STORE NEAR YOU.

Be there.

Jessica

I couldn't get to the girls' bathroom until the long break after second period. Fortunately it was empty. I went over to the sink and splashed a little water on my face.

Kristin came in. Obviously she was looking for me. I turned away, willing myself not to burst into tears.

Kristin put a hand on my shoulder. "Listen . . ."

I shrugged off her hand. "How could you tell Lacey everything?" I demanded. "You promised."

"I know. I'm sorry. I . . ."

One thing I'd learned about Sweet Valley Junior High, the girls here were tougher than my old crowd. Meaner too. They probably felt like they'd won if they could make you cry.

Well, I wasn't going to let them win anymore.

Kristin pulled out a towel and held it out to me so I could dry my face. "Here."

I ignored it, reached past her, and pulled out my own towel. "I don't want anything from you. I can take care of myself."

She sighed. "You don't understand."

"Yes, I do. I told you all that stuff about Damon because I thought you were my friend."

"I *am* your friend."

"But of course, you told Lacey," I interrupted. "And now she's using it to try and take him away from me."

Kristin looped her thumbs under the shoulder straps of her backpack. "What do you mean? I was only trying to help!"

I finished drying off my face and threw away the towel. "Forget it."

"No, wait. I told Lacey because I thought it would turn her *off* of Damon," she started to explain.

"I *said* forget it. Okay? Why don't you just do me a favor and leave me alone?"

Kristin backed up toward the door.

"Lacey told me she was going to make a big play for Damon to get Gel jealous. I thought the baby-sitting thing would make her back off. Lacey *hates* to baby-sit. Her little sister drives her nuts. I—I really was trying to help you."

"Yeah, right," I retorted. "Help me by telling Lacey stuff I told you not to tell anyone? Stuff that Damon probably doesn't want anybody to know? You know Lacey hates me."

Jessica

Kristin glanced at her watch. "Look. I gotta go. Can we talk later?"

I shook my head. What did we have to talk about?

Obviously if it came down to me or Lacey, Lacey would come first in Kristin's eyes. If that meant she had to betray me to keep Lacey happy, then she was ready and willing to drop me in the dirt.

"I'm sorry," she said quietly. "I really am." Then she left.

I rested my forehead against the cool bathroom tile and closed my eyes. I couldn't believe it. I'd come to school today feeling so up. Ready to let Damon know I really liked him. Feeling like things were changing. But the truth was, nothing was changing at all. Every time I thought I was taking a step in the right direction, I wound up falling on my face.

I took one last look in the mirror to see if I had *idiot* written across my forehead. I should have for thinking I could *ever* trust Kristin.

I left the bathroom and practically ran to my locker. I had maybe two minutes before the class bell rang. My hands were shaking so much, I could hardly get my locker open. When would I learn that I couldn't trust anyone at this stupid school? When?

I turned my head and saw Damon at his locker, about five feet away.

I remembered what I set out to do today—look the guy in the eye and say hello. No way was that happening now. Not after he'd gone out with Lacey. Who knew what she'd told him about me? What if he didn't say hello back? What if he just looked right through me?

I'd die.

I turned away and pretended to rearrange my books in my backpack. The best thing to do was to avoid all eye contact with Damon Ross.

Forever.

LUNCH

12:00 P.M.   Damon decides to take the plunge and go into the cafeteria. Now that he's got sort of a friendship going with Lacey, maybe he could sit with her. And maybe Kristin and Jessica might join them.

12:03 P.M.   Lacey sits out on the steps, hoping to bump into Damon, and so she won't have to face Kristin in the cafeteria.

12:05 P.M.   Kristin sits in the library so she won't have to face Jessica or talk to Lacey.

12:06 P.M.   Jessica sits in the last stall in the girls' bathroom so she won't have to face anybody.

12:10 P.M.   Damon takes a place at Lacey and Kristin's usual table in the cafeteria—by himself—but no one comes along to join him. He begins to wish he'd gone to his usual spot on the front steps. At least it was quieter and didn't smell of egg salad.

12:15 P.M. Halfway through her sandwich, Lacey has finished an apology note to Kristin. Complete with "tear" stains, which are really droplets of diet Sprite, carefully applied with a straw.

12:20 P.M. Jessica decides she should be ashamed of herself, sitting in the bathroom during lunch period. She gathers what's left of her lunch and her courage and marches out of the bathroom toward the cafeteria.

12:21 P.M. Lacey inserts the note into the slats of Kristin's locker and waits in the classroom across the hall for Kristin to gather her books for the afternoon.

12:23 P.M. Kristin finishes lunch early and goes to her locker. She finds Lacey's note and starts reading.

12:24 P.M. Damon grabs a candy bar from the vending machine, sits back down at Kristin and Lacey's table, and takes a huge bite out of the candy bar. Jessica appears at the cafeteria door. Damon looks up and struggles to call out "hello" but can't quite manage it around the caramel and peanut butter binding his jaw shut.

12:25 P.M.   Kristin finishes Lacey's note. Reflecting on how miserable Lacey's home life is, she breaks down and begins to cry. Lacey emerges from the classroom. Lacey and Kristin hug and promise to be best friends forever.

12:26 P.M.   Jessica runs from the cafeteria, wiping tears from her eyes. She can't believe Damon was sitting at Lacey's table! Are the two of them sharing their lunch periods now? She turns the corner to go to her locker and witnesses Kristin and Lacey's hug. She wonders why someone doesn't just shoot her.

Lacey

"Kristin is here," Penelope announced on Friday evening. I glanced up from filing my nails. Penelope hovered in the doorway like she wasn't sure if I was going to thank her for the announcement or scream at her to get lost. I noticed she was still clutching the bright bear I'd given her.

I felt too good to scream at anybody. So I hopped off my bed, gave her a pat on the head, and bounded downstairs.

Kristin was standing in the living room with this really serious look on her face.

"What's up?" I asked.

"I need to talk to you," she said.

"Okay. Let me get some sodas, and we'll go upstairs."

I was glad Kristin wanted to talk. I'd sobbed on her shoulder enough lately. It was time I returned the favor.

Moments later we were up in my room with the door closed. Kristin flopped down into the beanbag chair, and I sat on the floor with my back against the foot of my bed. I took a sip of soda. "So? What's the trouble?"

"Look—I've been thinking a lot about this. I never should have told you the stuff Jessica told me about Damon. So that part is definitely my fault. I'm not blaming you."

I tried to keep my face neutral, but I felt a stab of anger. *Jessica. Again!* I thought I had taken care of that problem.

Kristin leaned forward. "But I do blame you for using that information to hurt one of my friends."

"I am not *trying* to hurt Jessica Wakefield," I said, and took a long swig of soda. "I don't even care about her."

Kristin didn't look convinced. "Well, you're using Damon to make Gel jealous. And that's not fair to Damon."

"That's not true," I argued. "I *like* Damon. More than I thought I would. He's good company. And in case you haven't noticed, he's drop-dead gorgeous."

Kristin continued. "And anyway, I'm really mad about you taking me totally for granted. You don't care what kind of trouble you get me into as long as you get what *you* want."

"What? That is so not true," I defended myself. "I totally care."

"I thought you'd say that. Why don't you prove it, then?"

"How?"

"Apologize to Jessica and quit picking on her. Stop trying to sabotage my friendship with her."

"Apologize—to *Jessica*?" I sputtered. "No way! I didn't do anything to her."

"Come on, Lacey. She won't even speak to me now. And it's partly your fault."

"Look, if Jessica didn't want anybody to know what she found out about Damon, she shouldn't have told. If you ask me, she's just overreacting—probably to get your attention. If I were you, I'd keep my distance. Honestly, Kristin, that girl is too high maintenance."

Kristin's eyebrows rose to somewhere up around her hairline. "Excuse me!" she said. "If I dropped all of my high-maintenance friends, you would be the first to go."

"Hey!" I yelped. "That is so unfair."

"It is not!" Kristin argued. "You have this . . . this *need* to talk about yourself all the time. And if you're not talking about *you*, you're obsessing about Gel, which is totally boring. I mean, all you do is complain about him, when I know for a fact that you really like him. And . . . and . . ." She didn't finish, but I knew what she was going to say.

"Come on. Not the homework thing again?" I asked.

She nodded. "You know how I hate it. But you keep asking me anyway. Face it, Lacey, you just don't care about me. At all."

I felt bad. Kristin was a lot madder at me than I'd realized. If I didn't redeem myself soon, I was going to be without a best friend.

"I'm sorry," I said immediately. "I'm *really* sorry. I didn't realize how selfish I've been lately. I'll change. I promise I will."

"It's really simple, Lacey. Your happiness doesn't *have* to depend on other people's misery. Just think about *other* people every once in a while. People like me. Or like Jessica."

Jessica!

In spite of everything that we'd talked about I still felt enraged every time Kristin mentioned her name. But I wasn't going to tell Kristin that. "What do you want me to say to Wakefield?" I asked in my most exhausted tone.

"Just tell her you're sorry. You shouldn't have teased her after what you overheard in the bathroom. And you shouldn't be giving her such a hard time. And you should never have used information that you knew was confidential to make friends with Damon."

I nodded. "Okay. Okay. I'll tell her all that. I

promise." But behind my back, my fingers were tightly crossed. No way was I going to apologize to Jessica Wakefield. For anything.

Kristin gave me a little wary smile.

I smiled back. "Are we cool now? Best friends forever?"

"We're cool—on a strictly probationary basis. We'll see what happens in the next couple of weeks."

She leaned back in the beanbag chair again. "So, what time do you want to go to Pirate's Ice Cream Cove tomorrow? Eleven? Twelve? I've got to be home by two."

The question hit me like a bucket of cold water.

Tomorrow? I was going with Damon to see Jim Squalor at the mall tomorrow!

I'd completely forgotten about my ice-cream date with Kristin.

How was I going to get out of it?

I wanted to parade around the mall with Damon while Gel watched. Not sit in the ice-cream parlor pigging out with Kristin and wearing some stupid eye patch.

"Oh no!" I snapped my fingers like I had just remembered something. "I completely forgot. It's my aunt's birthday tomorrow. We're supposed to go visit her. Dad reminded me this morning, and I forgot to tell you."

"But—it's our anniversary."

"I know. But for some reason, Dad's being, like, totally rigid about it." I shrugged. "Sorry. Maybe we could change our anniversary to *next* Saturday?" I felt pretty terrible doing this, especially after everything we'd just talked about. But I couldn't give up my one shot to get Gel back for ice cream. That didn't make sense.

Kristin sighed. "Sure. No problem. My mom's been wanting me to help her clean my closet. It'll be a good day to do it. Nothing else is going on except that Jim Squalor thing at the mall." She rolled her eyes. "I can't believe the number of people who are psyched up for that."

I had a sudden moment of panic. "You wouldn't *go* to something like that, would you?"

She waved her hand. "Are you kidding? The guy is vile."

As I walked Kristin down the steps and out to the front door, I'd never felt quite so guilty in my life. I'd told her a big lie about where I would be tomorrow. And I had no intention of apologizing to Jessica.

But Kristin would forgive me when it was all over.

Because if it all went according to plan, there was a happy ending in it for everybody.

Gel would see me there with Damon, looking like we were totally in love. Gel would get jealous and beg me to come back.

Then I'd give Damon a push. And I'd be sure to do it in Jessica's direction. If she wanted my seconds, she could have them, for all I cared.

And then everyone would be happy.

How could Kristin get mad about that?

She'd be *congratulating* me. I'd make sure of it.

Damon

"What a fantastic day!" Lacey and I were standing in front of the mall. I threw back my head and took a deep breath. The weather was warm, but cool enough for a little exercise. "What do you say we ditch Jim Squalor and take a walk instead?"

A slightly panicked look crossed Lacey's face. "In these shoes?" She held up one foot. "No way!"

I blushed. How stupid. I should have noticed her shoes right away. They were these really high, platform-clog things. Not exactly your ideal walking footwear.

"Come on." She tugged at my arm. "It'll be fun. Jim Squalor has a certain gruesome charm."

"Uhh—sure," I agreed. "Let's go." We headed through the sliding-glass doors and into the marble front entry of the mall.

The truth was, I wasn't real excited about spending my free time with a big crowd of the same people I saw at school every day. I was

106

used to taking Saturdays for myself.

Still, I'd agreed to go. Lacey was obviously going out of her way to be friends with me, even though I had given her absolutely no reason to want to. So what was my problem?

"Do you think I'm ridiculous for wanting to see this?" she asked me.

I shook my head. "No. No way."

I really didn't. If Lacey liked to be where the action was, that was great. I usually avoided scenes like this. But maybe it was time to branch out a little.

As we walked into the mall, I kept my eyes open for Jessica. I couldn't help frowning slightly when I thought about her. Over the last few days I couldn't even get her to look at me. I wished I knew why. Was she totally avoiding me? Or was it just my imagination?

"Hello? Damon?"

I realized Lacey had been talking to me and I wasn't even listening. "Sorry. I just remembered something about one of my sisters. No big deal." I changed the subject. "So, you think lots of people from school will be here?"

"What does that matter—so long as the *right* people are here." Lacey grabbed my arm and kind of hugged it. She leaned in close to me. Really close. Like, I could feel her shirt on my arm and smell the perfume she was wearing. She gave me this look—this eyes-half-closed gaze. It was really, really sexy.

Whoa!

Why was Lacey looking at *me* that way? It took me a minute to get over my shock. But I slowly started to figure things out. Lacey had a reason to want to hang out with me, all right—it was because she wanted to be more than friends!

The thought hit me like a ton of bricks. How did this happen? How did I not see this coming? My stomach did a little flip-flop. Oh, man. I didn't like Lacey *that* way. Did she think I did?

The last few days flashed through my mind. We *had* spent that afternoon at the mall together, which was more time than I'd ever spent with anyone else at school—that was for sure. I had almost hugged her good-bye too. I mean, I always hug my sisters and my mom. But I decided not to. Now that I thought about it, Lacey *was* always kind of touching me when we talked. You know, putting her hand on my arm or my knee. And I guess I never stopped her.

Man! Of course she thinks I like her.

My mind raced on. What if other people saw us together and thought the same thing Lacey did? My breath caught in my chest. What if *Jessica* thought that?

Whoa! If Jessica thought I was interested in Lacey, it might explain a lot. Like why she wasn't looking at me the way she did before. Somehow I had to tell her she was getting the wrong picture—totally.

But how could I set her straight about my love life when I didn't even know her well enough to say, "How are you?"

I snapped out of my thoughts and glanced over at Lacey. She was turning her head right and left, as if she was looking for someone. Several people waved and said hello. Lots of people from the high school were there. Lacey threaded her arm through mine.

I started to sweat. Her hanging on my arm like that seemed too . . . I don't know . . . *intimate*. I felt totally uncomfortable.

I started to spot people from SVJH as we got near the platform, where there was a big sign announcing the appearance of Jim Squalor.

We moved through the crowd until we couldn't get any closer. I wound up standing right next to Brian Rainey. I knew him from Spanish class.

He smiled at me. "How ya doin'?"

I nodded. "Okay. You?"

Damon

"Don't know yet. This isn't really my kind of show. But my brother thinks this guy is great."

The tall guy with Brian turned and nodded at me. "Hey, I'm Billy. And yes, I have terrible taste in DJs. But don't worry. I'm getting counseling."

I laughed. "I'm Damon. Glad you're seeking help."

Lacey nodded at them. "So what's the deal? Where's the famous shock jock?"

"I guess he's late," Brian answered.

Even though Brian and I had never really spoken at school, it felt stupid not to make conversation now. "You ever see this guy before?" I asked him.

Brian shook his head. "No. And we had to sneak out to come. We were afraid my little sister would want to come with us. If Mom heard her walking around the house giving everybody the Squalor Holler, she'd kill us."

I laughed. "Oh, man! My sister's four. She repeats everything I say. I have to be very, very careful."

"Damon has *two* sisters," Lacey said. She squeezed my arm. "That's sort of how we got together." Lacey looked up and smiled. Then she squeezed my arm. *Again!*

That settled it. Lacey definitely had the wrong idea about what we were doing here. And I didn't have a clue what to do about it.

I glanced over at Brian and his brother, Billy. Man, I wished I had a big brother. I could have used a little male advice at this point.

I swept my eyes over the crowd. The first floor around the stage was pretty much full. I checked out the upper level. People had started gathering up there to get a bird's-eye view.

That's when I spotted Jessica. She was standing with her sister, looking down over the rail.

I could hear Lacey, Brian, and Billy talking, but it was hard to focus on the conversation. I couldn't stop staring at Jessica. I was so afraid she might look down, see me with Lacey, and get the wrong idea—again.

I wished I had told Lacey I couldn't come. I wished I'd never tried to be friends.

Something Brian said broke through the thoughts buzzing in my head. "You into sports?" he asked.

I was so distracted, I fell right into the trap. "Uhh—sure. You bet. Football. Hockey. Basketball."

"Yeah? How come you don't try out for one of the teams?"

I felt like kicking myself. Exactly the kind of conversation I didn't want to have. "No time," I answered.

"It's only three afternoons a week."

"Yeah, but—" I broke off. Did I really want to admit that I had to baby-sit weekday afternoons because it was just me and my mom at home and we couldn't afford day care?

"The hockey team could use you," Brian pressed.

"I've got a bad knee," I lied. "From playing hockey back at my old school. It sounds lame, but I'd be pretty useless on any team."

"Bummer," Brian said.

"That's okay. Damon has better things to do after school," Lacey said. She leaned against me. Suddenly I was so hot and so nervous, I just wanted to get out of there.

But I couldn't. I was trapped.

Jessica

"Why are we here again?" Elizabeth asked.

"I don't know," I said.

"Would you cheer up?" Elizabeth poked my arm. "This is supposed to be fun, right?"

"No," I answered glumly. "What's the point of cheering up? There's nothing to be cheerful about."

"How can you say that when *the* Jim Squalor is going to be appearing any minute?" she joked in a mock-excited voice. "It's, like, the thrill of a lifetime."

We leaned over the second-floor rail, looking down at the crowd. I saw lots of people from school. And lots of high-school people. Some friends of our older brother, Steven. And some people who had been at our semisuccessful, semidisastrous party a few weeks back. The party had been my attempt at a social life. It had gone well until Lacey tried to ruin it by bringing Gel and a bunch of thugs.

I should have realized then that Lacey was going to dedicate the rest of her life to destroying mine. "I can't believe we actually came to the mall for Jim Squalor," I muttered.

"We didn't," Elizabeth reminded me. "We came because you said everybody else would be here and you didn't want to look like a stay-at-home loser."

"Did I say that?"

"Yes."

"Well, I wish I had stayed home because being here just makes me feel like more of a loser. No offense, but hanging on to my sister isn't really making me look that good. It's sort of like going to the prom with your cousin."

Elizabeth laughed. "Why is your sense of humor always so much better when you're miserable?"

"Because when I'm miserable, it's all I've got," I answered. "And it doesn't seem to be getting me anywhere either."

"Why didn't you call Kristin?" Elizabeth asked.

"Kristin and I are finished," I muttered. "She didn't turn out to be the kind of friend I thought. She's probably somewhere with Lacey."

"Uhh—not today," Elizabeth said. "Because there's Lacey."

114

I followed the line of Elizabeth's finger and gasped.

There was Lacey, *standing right next to Damon Ross*. The sight of them together made my stomach turn. Lacey had her hand on Damon's arm. Then she leaned against him.

Damon's gaze met mine. I couldn't look away. Our eyes locked.

I could hear the PA come to life with a horrible squeal. "And now, ladies and gentlemen, the king of the airwaves—the indisputable ruler of radio—Jim Squalor!"

The crowd let out a roar and surged forward. Damon fought to keep his place, still looking up. Looking up at me.

"Want to go down there?" Elizabeth asked.

I couldn't answer. Because I couldn't tear my eyes away.

Lacey

The idiots in the crowd started roaring for Jim Squalor. But they might as well have been roaring for me. This day was going even better than I had dreamed.

Almost every single person at school had seen me with Damon Ross. And a lot of those people knew Gel or knew Gel's friends.

Word of my new "boyfriend" would be back to Gel by this afternoon. That is, if he didn't see me and Damon with his own eyes.

And if I knew Gel, my phone would be ringing by the time I walked in the front door.

I looked up at Damon—the guy who'd made all this possible. He was just the greatest. So handsome. So cool.

Then something strange happened. When I looked at him, my heart actually fluttered. For real. I might have actually felt romantic if about three hundred guys weren't joining Jim Squalor in the Squalor Holler.

Brian and his brother were into it. But Damon

didn't seem to be paying any attention. He was looking up at something. I started to look up too. And that's when I saw Gel.

He was standing near the platform speaker. And he was with a girl! A gorgeous girl. An older girl. A girl who was almost better looking than me.

My heart just stopped. I couldn't believe it.

His arm was draped casually over her shoulders, like they had been dating a long time.

Had they? Had Gel been seeing her when he was still with me? Gel looked in my direction, his eyes idly scanning the crowd. I could just feel his gaze about to lock on me.

"Show time," I whispered to myself.

A split second before Gel could make eye contact, I looked up at Damon, put my arms around him, and pulled his head down toward mine.

Damon

It happened so fast, I didn't know what to do.

One second I was standing there listening to the Squalor Holler. The next second Lacey was kissing me—right there in the middle of the crowd!

Like, for *real*. Her lips were on mine, her arms were around me, and her shoulders were hunched up against my chest.

And Jessica was watching!

I had to fight the urge to push Lacey away. I had to fight the urge to run.

Somehow I managed to unwind her arms from around my neck. "Uh, Lacey," I whispered, "let's go outside." I didn't want to make a scene; I just wanted to get her somewhere more private so I could tell her I liked her as a *friend*. I was afraid her feelings would be hurt. This wasn't going to be easy.

She didn't resist or argue, but she slipped her hand in mine as we walked out of the crowd and toward the exit. All around us Jim Squalor's voice resounded over the PA system.

"All right, metal heads. It's a beautiful day. I feel beautiful, so beautiful, I could *scream!*"

Suddenly everyone in the mall was screaming at the top of their lungs. I couldn't wait to get out of there.

Outside, in the daylight, Lacey gave me a crooked smile and raised one brow. "Surprised?"

"Uh. Yeah." I took a step back, afraid she might try to kiss me again.

She took a step forward. "*Pleasantly* surprised?"

I hoped what I was about to say wouldn't seem insulting. "Well . . . ummm . . . not exactly."

The smile immediately left her face, and her forehead wrinkled darkly. "What?"

I pointed over to a low wall outside the entrance. "Let's sit down and talk, okay?"

I sat down, and she sat beside me. "I like you a lot, Lacey. But only as a *friend*."

She stared at me like she couldn't believe what she was hearing. "*What?*" she hissed.

My stomach began to knot. "Please don't be angry."

She laughed. It was a harsh sound.

"Angry? You think I'm angry?" She took a

119

cigarette out of her purse. Her hands were trembling as she lit it and lowered her eyelids.

"Aren't you?" I asked.

She expelled a stream of smoke. "I don't get angry with guys—I get even. You want to know the truth? I've been using you. To get another guy. So don't feed your ego. Okay?"

I felt like I had been slapped. How did this turn so ugly, so fast? All of a sudden Lacey was looking at me like I was some kind of worm.

My throat tightened. I'd been given that look before—although it was for a different reason.

I wasn't about to sit there and take it.

I stood up. "I'm going home."

Lacey's face suddenly just—crumpled. That's the only way I can explain it.

She threw down her cigarette, and her hands flew to her eyes. It didn't help. I could see the tears leaking through them anyway.

I did the only thing I could think of. I pulled her against me and pressed her head on my shoulder. "It's okay," I said, patting her back. It's what I do with my sisters when they cry, and it usually works. So I just kept patting and saying, "It's okay. It's okay."

"Do you think I'm horrible?" she sobbed. "Everybody else does."

"No. I don't think you're horrible."

She took a deep breath. "But I *am* horrible," she said in a shaking voice. She sat up and wiped her eyes with the hem of her T-shirt.

"Gel broke up with me, and I just wanted to get him back. So I figured if he saw me with you—" She swallowed hard. "I wanted him to think I liked you so he'd get jealous." She sniffled. "I am so pathetic!"

I stared off into the parking lot—processing.

Lacey was using me in a little scheme to get her boyfriend back. That wasn't exactly what you'd call nice. But when I thought about it, she was just upset about losing her boyfriend, right? Don't people always say that love makes you do crazy things? I mean, who could blame her for that?

Then I remembered all of Lacey's questions that I avoided in the last few days. All the little white lies I had told.

Was the way I acted really any better than the way Lacey did?

"Listen. You really shouldn't feel bad," I told her.

"Oh yeah? Why not?"

"Because—well—I haven't exactly been telling you the truth either." I paused for a second— and decided to go through with it. "Do you know where I live?"

121

Lacey fished around in her purse. "I don't know." She sniffed vaguely. "Somewhere around school, I guess."

"I live in Briggs Heights," I told her.

Her hand paused for a moment. Then she pulled out a tissue and blew her nose. "So your dad's not a CEO. What's that have to do with anything?"

I looked her in the eyes. "It's not that my dad's not a CEO. My dad's MIA. He walked out on us years ago. My mom is a waitress. We live in a mobile home—a *trailer.* And sometimes it feels like we have absolutely *no* money. I baby-sit because we can't afford day care."

I stopped. Lacey kept staring at me. She didn't say a word.

Did she get it? Did she understand what I was telling her? That I hadn't exactly given her the whole picture either. And I probably wasn't someone she or anyone else like her would want to date. Including Jessica.

I felt my face turn red. I knew what was going on here. Lacey was speechless—because she'd never talked to trailer trash before.

She was judging me—just like everyone else—by where my family lived and how they lived, without even knowing the whole story.

Well, she didn't have to talk to trailer trash ever again.

"Forget it, Lacey." I hopped off the wall. "Have a good life."

I started walking toward home. Toward Briggs Heights. It wasn't much of a neighborhood. But at least I didn't have to explain anything to the people who lived there. And I didn't have to apologize for who I was.

"Damon! Damon! Wait!"

I turned. Lacey was running after me—or trying to in those high-heeled things.

I stood still.

When she caught up, she opened and closed her mouth a few times, like she was trying to think of something to say.

Then she kissed me. On the cheek this time. Like a friend. Not putting on a show.

"I already knew all that stuff—about the trailer. But I don't judge people like that. At least, I don't judge them by the usual standards."

I felt my shoulders stiffen. "What?" Did *everybody* know where I lived? Was I an idiot, thinking I could keep it a secret all this time?

"But you should know the truth about me too," Lacey went on. "There's no way of making this sound nice, so . . . I'm not a nice, devoted big sister," she blurted out. "She's my stepmother's

123

daughter—I can't stand her. But I heard you did a lot of baby-sitting, so I engineered the whole conversation on the steps. It wasn't my sister's birthday—I wouldn't have cared if it was. I just wanted an excuse to spend some time with you. I made all that stuff up so you would go to the mall with me."

"Why?" I asked, dumbfounded.

She smiled crookedly. "What are you, dense? I already told you. To make Gel jealous."

"But—why me?"

"Well, you *are* gorgeous," she said matter-of-factly, in the same voice she might have pointed out that my shirt was blue.

I started walking, and Lacey fell in step beside me.

"So, was Gel there today?" I asked. "When you gave me the big kiss?"

She nodded, her face looking like she was going to cry again. "Yes. But with another girl. A beautiful girl." Lacey moaned. "If I'm a ten, she's a twenty. I've lost him."

"Well, maybe he's just playing the same game you are," I volunteered.

Lacey's mouth popped open. I chuckled. I mean, I could just see the wheels turning.

"That's *true*," she muttered. "But why would anybody like that go out with Gel? He's such a jerk."

I was confused. "Then why do *you* want to go out with him?" I asked.

She rolled her eyes. "Because I'm nuts—and he's *my* jerk. Besides, he's got a car."

She didn't have to explain. I could tell she really liked him. "I hope you get him back," I told her solemnly.

We got to Lacey's bus stop.

"Will you be all right?" I asked her. "Want me to take you home?"

"I'll be okay," she said. "Go on. I know you've got stuff to do."

"All right," I said. But I didn't want to just take off. Something she'd said had really bugged me. "Listen," I added. "I never got along so well with my dad, you know? But I never took it out on my little sisters. They're just kids. You should give your sister a chance, okay?"

Lacey just nodded, staring at the ground like she was going to start crying again.

"Hey," I said. "Even though things got screwed up—thanks for getting to know me. People don't make much of an effort to be my friend."

She lifted her head and smiled. "You don't make much of an effort to be available."

Lacey was right. But that probably wasn't going to change. I'd stepped out of my own little circle, and it had been a pretty rough ride. I wasn't sure I wanted a whole lot more contact with the outside world just yet. "Thanks for a nice day. Thanks for two nice days."

She lifted her hand and turned down her street.

I took a couple of steps toward Briggs Heights, then suddenly stopped. "Hey! Lacey!"

She turned.

"How did you find out about me? About where I lived and the baby-sitting and everything?"

She shrugged. "Jessica Wakefield told Kristin Seltzer, and Kristin told me," Lacey said. Then she waved again and started home.

I stood there, rooted to the pavement.

Jessica? She *knew* about me? But how? I hadn't told a single person at school about my family until this afternoon. My stomach clenched. Here I was, thinking Jessica wouldn't look at me because of Lacey. But the truth was, Jessica just wasn't interested. And now I knew why. I guess she didn't want to have to hurt my feelings by turning me down, so she was trying to keep me at a distance.

Well, it was working.

How To Clean Out Your Closets and Ruin a Forever Friendship in Seven Easy Steps

STEP 1:   Kristin helps her mother clean out closets. She throws away: about five hundred ten-year-old head shots left over from her mother's modeling career, piles of resumes left over from countless job searches in the last ten years, and boxes of newspaper and magazine clippings with titles like . . . "Making Your Career Happen."

STEP 2:   Kristin reassures her mother that she is very capable and competent. It just takes time to find the right job and settle in.

STEP 3:   Kristin looks at her mother's old modeling portfolio. Four covers of *Vogue*. Three covers of *Harper's Bazaar*. And over a hundred fashion and makeup layouts. Kristin looks around their cramped apartment and vows to get a college education—no matter what.

STEP 4:   Too late. Kristin realizes they have filled five trash bags with debris and have no twist ties. She offers to run down to the store and get some.

STEP 5: Kristin walks into a convenience store and bumps into Brian Rainey (aka number one on Kristin's cute-guy list). She stops to talk and finds out that he's going to the mall to see Jim Squalor. Kristin thinks maybe she'll peek her head into the mall for a few minutes to check out the scene. She arranges to meet Brian there in half an hour.

STEP 6: Kristin walks around, trying to find Brian. She does find him—standing right by Lacey and Damon, whose lips are glued together in the middle of the mall.

STEP 7: As she runs home, angry tears streaming down her face, Kristin swears not to talk to Lacey Frells ever again for the rest of her natural life.

Lacey

Thanks to my pal Damon, I was actually in a pretty good mood when I got home. Maybe he was right. Maybe Gel's girl was a fake.

I hurried up to my room and closed the door. I didn't feel like talking to Victoria or Penelope. I didn't feel like talking to anybody. I needed to think. But then the phone rang. I thought maybe it was Gel, so I picked it up. "Hello?"

"How was your aunt's birthday?" Kristin asked me in a frosty, sarcastic tone.

Uh-oh.

My plan had been to report the afternoon's activities to Kristin before anyone else could. I'd explain that even though I'd lied to her, I had done it in order to arrange a happy ending for her new best buddy, Jessica. Which is not really what I intended—but sometimes you have to use what you've got.

But she'd called me first. And she obviously knew I'd lied.

I didn't have a plan B.

"Listen, Kristin," I began.

"You wouldn't believe what I've been hearing," she said in this sarcastic, sweet voice. "I don't know how these rumors get started . . . but people are saying that you and Damon were at the mall. And that you were all over each other. Isn't that *funny!*"

"I'm sorry," I said. "I can explain."

Kristin dropped the sweet sarcasm. "You don't need to," she snapped. "I already know everything I need to know. I *saw* you. You lied to me."

"I know. I know. But I was trying to get Gel back, and . . . please don't be mad," I begged. "You're my best friend."

"You're sick, Lacey. Really. You don't know how to be a friend. To you everyone is just a prop in your own personal drama—aren't they?"

"That's not true."

"Yes, it is. And I'm tired of it. I don't need friends who lie to me and use me."

I could feel tears in my eyes now. Kristin had never said such—such mean things to me before. And I'd never heard her use that tone of voice. She sounded like she hated me.

"I'm sorry," I said softly.

"You gave me a piece of good advice the other day, Lace. You told me I should drop my high-maintenance friends," Kristin paused. "So I'm taking your advice."

"Please don't," I begged.

"Good-bye," Kristin said.

She hung up the phone. She didn't bang it or anything. But it was the loudest, loneliest sound I have ever heard.

I sat down on the floor of my room and dropped my head in my hands. What was I going to do? What?

I tried to be quiet, but I couldn't stop sobbing. I didn't want Victoria or Dad to hear me. I just wasn't up to explaining the situation. They loved Kristin and hated Gel. No matter what I told them about what happened, I'd wind up getting a lecture on how bad my judgment was.

And for once, Victoria and Dad would be right.

Suddenly I sensed someone standing beside me. Just standing quietly. I lifted my head. It was Penelope, watching me with big, sad eyes. She had the Day-Glo bear under one arm.

Penelope didn't say a word, but she put her other arm around my neck and squeezed. It was the nicest hug. I think it's the first time she ever hugged me.

"Thank you." I sniffed. I pulled her into my lap.

"Did you fall down?" Penelope asked me solemnly. "Are you hurt?"

I nodded. "Kind of."

Penelope hesitated a moment, then she held up the bear. It was half smushed and had a wad of cotton sticking out through a torn seam.

"Bear fell down too," Penelope said quietly. "I dropped him in the driveway, and Mom ran over him. She said it was an accident."

I couldn't help it. I started to giggle. I took the bear from her and tried to push the cotton back inside. "Don't worry," I said. "Everybody gets knocked around a little sometimes. Bear will be all right."

And, I hoped, so would I.

Jessica

"Would you please cheer up?" Elizabeth moaned at me.

"Didn't we have this conversation before?" I asked grumpily.

"It seems like it's the *only* conversation we ever have." Elizabeth sighed. "Couldn't you at least *try* to smile?"

"If you were me, would you be smiling?"

"No," Elizabeth said quietly. "I wouldn't. I'm sorry, Jessica. I didn't realize how much you liked him."

"It's not *only* that. It's everything. Everything I've tried to do since we started at Sweet Valley Junior High just blows up in my face."

Elizabeth gave me a sympathetic look.

It was Monday, and we were riding the bus to school. I'd felt so miserable that morning, I could hardly get dressed. Watching Damon and Lacey kiss like that and then leave together . . . It was like a knife through my heart.

I couldn't believe I had ever thought Damon

might like me. How could I have been so incredibly stupid? The whole thing was so mortifying, I could die.

There was only one thing left to do. I'd have to move to another city. Change my name. Or at the very least, never go to school again.

"I'm going back home," I announced, standing up.

Elizabeth caught my arm. "Oh no, you don't. What would Mom say?"

"I'll sneak into the house," I insisted. "She'll never know I'm there."

"Yeah. Right. Your record for keeping quiet is what? Five minutes?"

"I can't go to school!" I insisted. "I can't face it. I can't face having no friends and being completely humiliated."

Elizabeth gave me a long, sympathetic look. "Jessica! I am your sister and your friend. It may not make you look like the popularity queen of school, but if it makes you feel any better, I'll hang with you all day."

I sighed and sat down.

I felt tears well up in my eyes. When we transferred, I never thought this would happen to me. If anything, I expected Elizabeth to have the adjustment problems. But she was handling everything fine.

It was me who couldn't cope.

"What's the matter with me?" I choked.

"Jessica," Elizabeth said quietly. "You're just finding out how ninety percent of the junior-high-school population feels."

I didn't say anything.

"At Sweet Valley Middle you were really popular. But you have to realize everyone feels insecure about their friends and where they fit in."

"Why don't you?"

"I do. I just try not to let it run my life. I think it's more important to be yourself, and if people aren't flocking to you, then that's their problem, not yours."

Would I ever be the kind of person who thinks like that? I wondered.

Probably not.

I wanted people to like me too much. When they didn't, I became a basket case.

"Come on," Elizabeth urged, standing up. "We're here."

Reluctantly I got to my feet. We made our way off the bus, and there it was. Sweet Valley Junior High.

The first bell hadn't rung yet, and lots of people were milling around out front.

I heard someone call my name.

"Jessica! Jessica! Wait! Please!"

I turned around and saw Kristin running

toward me. Panting, she caught up with me and Elizabeth. "Hi!"

"Hi," Elizabeth and I said together.

Kristin licked her lips. "Jessica, could I talk to you a minute? It's . . . umm . . ."

"I have to go to my locker," Elizabeth said quickly, catching on that Kristin had something private to tell me.

What could Kristin possibly have to say to me? "Yes?" I asked, staring at her.

Kristin bit her lip.

"What?" I demanded.

"I'm really sorry," Kristin said finally. "I want to apologize. For everything. For telling Lacey what you told me. For acting like you didn't have any right to be mad. And for underestimating what a *user* Lacey is."

I looked down. This was unbelievable.

"Look, Lacey used that baby-sitting information to make friends with Damon. And she's using Damon, I'm sure, to get back at Gel. She uses everybody. All the time. I've had enough, and I'm just sorry I didn't see this coming before you got hurt."

I didn't say anything. I couldn't think of anything to say. This was so unexpected.

So Kristin and Lacey weren't friends anymore. Where did that leave me?

Kristin's face was so earnest. She really wanted to make it up to me, I could tell. If I wanted to give our friendship a chance, I had to give her the benefit of the doubt.

"Sorry I got so mad at you before," I said.

"Don't worry. I would've been just as mad. It was stupid of me to tell Lacey. I'm just *so* sorry," Kristin answered.

"Forget about it," I said.

"Thanks." Kristin smiled gratefully.

"So," I said, getting my hopes up. "Then Lacey doesn't really like Damon, right?"

"I don't know." Kristin shrugged. "And who knows what she's told him."

I groaned. It would be just like Lacey Frells to tell Damon that I had followed him. No wonder Damon was staring at me at the mall. He hated my guts!

"I'm sorry," Kristin said. "I feel like I blew it for you."

I shook my head. "No, you didn't blow it. Just because I like Damon doesn't mean he likes me." I sighed. "I'm sorry I got so mad at you."

"It's okay," Kristin said. "Friends?" she asked.

I tried to smile. It was nice to know that Kristin really did care about me.

"Friends," I answered.

And side by side, we walked into school.

Suddenly, aside from Damon, I was feeling pretty okay.

My friend Bethel from the track team gave me a playful punch as she passed me in the hall. "Ready to run today?" she asked.

"You bet," I answered. "Ready to eat my dust?"

"As if!" Bethel laughed and walked on.

"Hey! Jessi-*cat!* What's happening?" It was Salvador del Valle. He drove me crazy with his stupid variations on my name. But it was a good-natured feud. The kind you had with people you were friends with.

"Not much, Sal-*ivator*," I shot back. That made him laugh. Kristin too.

I waved at Anna Wang. At Sheila Watson. I nodded hello to a guy from my English class.

All around me, I realized that the faces that had once seemed so cold and unfamiliar were now people I knew—or people I was getting to know.

I also realized that there were some pretty cute guys around this school. Lots. I took a deep breath.

Okay. Maybe Damon really liked Lacey, which meant he was no longer available. And maybe he hated my guts, which also meant he was no longer available. What I had to do was move on.

Get over it. Start looking for someone new and crush-worthy.

I saw Lacey walking toward us and felt Kristin stiffen beside me.

Lacey's face was pale and drawn. She gave Kristin a tentative smile as she got closer.

But Kristin turned her head away and walked right past her without saying a word.

Lacey's face fell. She seemed so rejected and hurt, I couldn't help it—I actually felt sorry for her.

Imagine that.

The thing is, her face looked the way I had been feeling since school started. And it was a lousy way to feel. I hoped I wouldn't feel that way again for a long, long time.

Lacey

"Hey! What's the matter?" Damon stopped beside my locker. "You look like you lost your best friend."

I smiled tightly. "As a matter of fact, I did."

There was a long pause. "Want to talk about it?"

I stared at Damon. His brow was furrowed, and his gorgeous face actually looked concerned. Concerned for me. But when you got right down to it, he was a guy. And I wasn't the kind of girl who had guy friends. I had boyfriends. Not guy friends.

Kristin had guy friends. Even Penelope had little mini–guy friends. Most girls had guy friends.

But I didn't think any guy could be the kind of friend I needed. I guess the truth is that I *am* a high-maintenance friend. I need a lot of attention. It's more than most guys are willing to give unless they have a crush on me.

Damon and I would be friendly. Sure. But we wouldn't talk every day. Or hang out all the time. He was too much of a loner. He couldn't take Kristin's place, that's for sure.

"Thanks," I said quietly. "But I just need to be by myself right now."

"Hey! Damon, my man!" Brian walked by and slapped a hand down on Damon's shoulder. "Going to math?"

"Do I have a choice?" Damon grinned.

"Not unless you're psyched for detention," Brian joked.

Damon laughed and waved good-bye, and the two guys walked off to math class together.

I felt glad for Damon. It looked like maybe he and Brian would turn out to be friends. One friend tended to lead to another. It was a chain.

But chains could break if you put enough pressure on them. I knew that from experience.

First and second periods seemed like they were four hours long. Finally the bell rang.

Kristin always had to go to her locker before third period so she could get her lab stuff. Her locker was in the East Hall, and I was in the West Hall.

When the bell rang, I just tore out of there. I think I may have even knocked a couple of people over.

"No running in the halls, Ms. Frells," I heard some teacher shout.

But I ignored him and careened around the corner.

I spotted Kristin just as she was about to close her locker. "Kristin! Wait!"

When she saw me, her face closed up a little.

I hurried toward her. "I have to talk to you."

"We have nothing to talk about."

"Yes, we do," I insisted. "I'm sorry. I'm really, really, really sorry. You're my best friend. I should never have used you the way I did. I shouldn't have used what you told me about Damon. I shouldn't have tried to hurt Jessica. And I shouldn't have lied to you."

"I thought our friendship was important," Kristin said. "But you just threw away our most special occasion so you could play games—with guys. To get Gel back."

"I'm sorry. I was completely wrong. But when it comes to guys, something weird happens to me. I just don't think. But I'll change."

"Don't change for me," she said curtly.

"I'm not changing for you," I said, realizing that what I was saying wasn't just baloney. "I'm going to change for *me*."

Kristin lifted her eyebrow, like she was very skeptical. She turned away and started walking off.

"Kristin! *Please!*" I could hear the grief in my voice. I guess Kristin could too.

When she turned toward me, her face was twisted as if she were in pain.

"Lacey! Why do you do this? How can I be your friend if you think it's okay to lie to me as long as you apologize afterward? It's not okay. It doesn't matter how sorry you are."

"But I *am* sorry." My lips were trembling. I didn't know if I could keep from crying.

"Don't *tell* me you're sorry. *Show* me you're sorry." I saw tears rolling off her cheeks.

"How?"

"Stop doing this stuff." She raked her sleeve across her face, wiping the tears away with a fierce gesture.

I put my hands over my face. "I'll try—just please don't walk away like that," I begged. "Please? I am so sorry." I sniffled.

Kristin's face seemed to soften a little bit then. Suddenly we were hugging.

"I know," she said.

"I *will* try to change. I promise. But—are we still friends?"

We broke apart and laughed at ourselves for getting so emotional. "Yeah, I'll still be your friend," she said. "On one condition."

"What's that?"

"You have to give me your eye patch on Saturday."

143

"No way!" I cried.

"Oh yeah," she said seriously. "It's mine. I want it."

"Okay, okay. It's yours."

She smiled. "Now we're even."

I watched her pull her math notebook out of her locker. I'd been so upset last night, I hadn't had time to do my math problems. For two seconds I was almost tempted to ask Kristin if I could copy hers.

One bad thing about having a really old friend—they can read your mind.

"Don't even think about it," she said, shoving the notebook down into her backpack.

I opened my eyes wide, trying to look completely innocent. "I wasn't."

"You were too," she countered.

"Was not," I said, bumping my hip against hers.

"Were too," she said.

We started giggling and walked arm and arm down the hall on our way to class. Laughing at our own silliness—just the way we had when we'd met in the second grade.

Gel's Six Reasons to
Get Back with Lacey

That girl from the arcade is so competitive.

Lacey never freaks out when I ask her to steer while I change the tape.

There's no one to drive around anymore.

My car looks good green.

Jim Squalor isn't that great anyway.

I like her.

Jessica

I almost fainted when I saw Kristin sitting with Lacey at lunch. I thought, *This can't be happening. It's some kind of nightmare. I'm crossing back and forth between parallel universes.*

In one universe Kristin is my friend.

In the other universe Kristin doesn't give me the time of day.

Which universe was this?

Kristin saw me hesitate at the door. She got up and hurried over to me. "Don't freak out," she said.

"What's going on?" I asked.

"Lacey and I made up."

I shook my head, trying to clear my thoughts.

"It's okay. It doesn't mean you and I aren't friends," Kristin insisted. "But Lacey and I are like sisters. We fight, but then we make up."

I thought about this. Elizabeth and I fight. All the time. But we always make up.

I took a deep breath. Okay. Maybe Kristin could really be Lacey's friend *and* my friend. I hoped so. But in the meantime I didn't want to have *anything* to do with Lacey Frells.

"Okay," I said. "You guys have a good lunch, and I'll see you later."

I headed toward another table, where Bethel and two other girls from the track team were sitting with Sheila Watson.

When she saw me coming, Bethel automatically pushed over to make room for me. That one little gesture made my whole day. My whole week.

Nobody made any big deal about my sitting down. They just said hello and kept on talking.

Sheila leaned forward. "I heard from Elsa that Innis Kay is going out with . . ."

I unpacked my lunch and prepared to enjoy the gossip.

It wasn't Sweet Valley Middle School. And it wasn't my old best friend, Lila, and our old crowd.

It was a new school with a new cast of characters.

And now—for the first time since I started here—I felt like a player.

Lacey Frells
English Composition
(revision)

Assignment: Write a paragraph starting with the phrase, "After high school . . ."

After high school I'm going to pack a suitcase full of my brightest clothes and go to college in a big city like New York. I'll drive my car back to Sweet Valley every once in a while, though, to see my little sister, Penelope.

Six Reasons Why I Wish Gel Would Call

1. I'm tired of walking.
2. There's no one to smoke with.
3. I don't really mind Jim Squalor.
4. He used to call me every night.
5. No one else calls me "babe."
6. I know he wants to call, and I'm sick of waiting.

A Page from
Damon Ross's Journal

October 19

Brian and I had a good talk on the way to class. We might even go to a game together sometime. I decided to come clean and tell him that I didn't have a lot of free time. That I had to baby-sit while my mom worked.

That was totally cool. He didn't even ask any questions.

That's the nice thing about guys like Brian. They just accept what you tell them. They don't need a lot of explanation. I don't know if it's because guys like that are just less curious about people in general. Or maybe he just likes to keep his own privacy, so he respects mine too. Anyway, it's cool.

I do know this—Lacey might be my friend, but she isn't going to be my best buddy or anything. I could tell she was uncomfortable with me today. I understand. We have kind of a weird history now anyway.

Brian mentioned Jessica once or twice. If they're friends . . . maybe I'll ask Brian what he thinks about "me and Jessica" someday.

But not now.

Jessica wouldn't even look at me today.

I decided not to take it personally. I'm used to not getting everything I want. Some toys are out of my price range. And some girls are out of my league.

That's life.

And life goes on.

Lacey

I was home doing my nails when the phone rang. I was pretty sure it was Kristin, so I picked it up on the first ring. "Hello?" I blew on my newly painted lime green thumbnail.

"Lacey?"

I was so startled, I smacked my thumbnail into my lip. Bleah! I could feel the polish cling. I probably looked like I had a great big lime green fever blister now.

"Hey."

"It's me, babe."

I sat up straighter and took a deep breath. Gel had sure taken his time. "What do you want?" I asked in a really cold voice.

"You, baby. I've never wanted anybody but you."

I could feel myself melting. Just melting away. Gel has this voice that . . . well . . . all I can say is just when I think I can't stand the sight of him for one more second, he'll say something in that tone of voice and I fall for him all over again.

"Gosh," I said. "You sure looked like you wanted somebody else at the mall on Saturday. Who was that?"

"Just some girl."

I smiled. Damon was right. Gel's gorgeous chick had been a fake. I couldn't resist putting him on the spot.

"Known her long?"

"A while."

"Dated her before?"

There was a long silence. "Look, Lacey, do you want to get back together or not?"

I flopped back against my pillows. It was so nice to be back in the driver's seat! "I don't know, Gel," I said. "I mean, it would be really hard to trust you after what happened."

"Come on, Lacey. You know you want to get back together."

"I don't know that at all," I replied, picking up my polish and going back to work on my nails. "I'll be honest. I met somebody."

"The guy at the mall?"

"You got it."

There was a long silence. I just knew Gel was picturing Damon and me kissing. And it was driving him wild.

"He's a pretty great guy. And he treats me well," I added.

"Okay. Okay. I acted like a jerk. But I'll change."

"I'm not sure you *can* change," I purred.

"Go out with me. Just once," he begged. "I'll show you. I'm a different guy now, Lace."

"I don't know. . . ."

"I had the car painted," he said.

That got my attention.

"What color?"

"Lime green. Because you said you liked it. You said it was your favorite color."

Well, what can I say? If a guy paints his car lime green because it's your favorite color, what can you do? You gotta go out with him? Right?

And if he didn't behave . . . Well, there was always Damon Ross to fall back on.

Kristin was right. I'll never change. I'm not even sure I want to.

So sue me.

Check out the **all-new** ....

Sweet Valley Web site—

www.sweetvalley.com

New Features

Cool Prizes

The **ONLY** official Web site!

Hot Links

And much more!

Bantam
Bantam Doubleday Dell

BFYR 217

You hate your alarm clock.

You hate your clothes.

You're going to love Jr. High.